THE BLACK HOLE

L. MARIE WOOD

OTHER MOCHA MEMOIRS HORROR TITLES

Dark Mocha Bites

Telecommuting by L. Marie Wood

Alice by Alledria Hurt

SLAY: Stories of the Vampire Noire edited by Nicole Givens Kurtz

Black Magic Women: 18 Stories by Scary Sisters edited by Sumiko Saulson

For Michael. You always believed in this one and now here it is. Hope it makes you smile.

1

"Damn man, gotta bring a nigga out to the boonies to play souped-up tag," Shaun said in his best thug impersonation as he looked through the fogged window of Martin's black Cherokee Limited Edition. It was cold that morning and he could see his breath in the air when he rolled down the window to get a better look outside.

"Shaun, what's up with the window? It's not like it's summer up in here," Martin said.

Shaun was too busy making faces and hand gestures at Gary, Kevin, and Robert in the forest green Jetta following behind them to pay attention to what Martin was saying. He was pointing out the horses grazing in the field on the right side of the car and shaking his head.

"Are you sure we're going the right way, Martin? I don't see any street signs," Craig asked as he looked curiously at the bales of hay neatly stacked on the driven land to the left of the car. He poked Shaun and said, "Are you seeing this shit? It's like we drove out of Maryland and into the backwoods of North Carolina!"

"I've followed the directions to the letter. They told me there wouldn't be any street signs. Nothing but farmland in sight for miles, they said," Martin picked up the crumpled piece of paper that had the directions on it and double-checked his steps. He had been invited to play 'Capture the Flag' by a guy he worked with. It was a dare, really. Martin had heard about the paintball craze before. A lot of the kids in his area seemed to like to do it on Friday nights with flashlights on their face masks. They would go into the woods and shoot at each other like crazy, until one of the teams surrendered. It was nothing but a little fad that the kids would soon be tired of, he thought. Nothing but a fad.

His co-worker, Jeremy, issued the paintball challenge to him one day during lunch. He said that he and a couple of his buddies go out every once in a while and horse around after work to shake the stress off. He said it was a lot of fun and a damned good release. *'Lord knows I could use that,'* Martin thought while Jeremy explained the rules to him. What Jeremy told him seemed to be a lot different than what he had heard before about paintball. He thought that playing paintball, or going paintballing, or whatever you called it, was nothing more than a kid's game. It certainly wasn't anything that he and his boys would want to do with their Saturday afternoons. Hoops was more like their speed - not pseudo-military combat with pretty little pink paint balls that splatter all over you on impact and color your clothes with water-solvent fluorescent paint. No, a real challenge was to take it to the hoop and slam it down somebody's throat. That's a game. That's sport. That's relaxing. It's what he and his boys did to shake the stress off.

Martin tried to explain the differences, both physical and mental, to Jeremy at lunch. For every point he brought up, Jeremy countered with another. It went on for almost the entire hour, both of their sandwiches going completely untouched. Finally, he said it. Jeremy issued the challenge.

"You want to try it? Your men against mine in the brush? I mean, that's if you can handle it," Jeremy said with a taunting smirk on his face. He sat back dramatically in his chair, satisfied with his lead. Jack, the controller who was sitting at another table, inched forward on Martin's pause. His forehead was peppered with sweat and his skin was furrowed with anticipation. Martin glanced over at Jack, and he looked away quickly, trying to act nonchalant. He began eating his sandwich slowly, his eyes darting towards Martin's table. Martin shook his head in amusement and turned back to Jeremy. Jack looked up from his sandwich and turned his attention to Jeremy and Martin's conversation again. He was listening, eagerly awaiting Martin's response. Martin was amazed at Jack's intrusion and tried to ignore it.

"You don't think I'll play, do you?"

Jeremy shrugged his shoulders theatrically.

"Would you come out to the court and sweat it up with the big boys," Martin asked. He didn't think that

Jeremy would bring his lily-white, country-club friends down to the gym to play b-ball with a bunch of Black guys. Not that he and his boys played ball in Southeast, DC, but anywhere in Chocolate City would scare the pants off the likes of Jeremy and his boys. It's a wonder Jeremy made it to work in Northwest without hyperventilating in his car.

Martin had met some of Jeremy's friends before. One day after work he and Jeremy met up with them in Georgetown for happy hour. They were in some hoity-toity bar where the drinks were extremely expensive and watered down. Places like that were always full of loose girls who were willing and able if you bought them enough drinks and patted them on the ass real nice. They flaunted their plastic surgeon's sculpted breasts in increments, teasing you with what could happen later, as long as the car you had parked outside was a BMW or a Porsche. Yeah, it was that kind of place.

Jeremy's friends Kurt, Chuck, and Brad came to the bar fifteen minutes after Martin and Jeremy arrived. Jeremy and his friends graduated from Georgetown University. Martin came out of Howard University. Even with four against one odds, a pretty heated discussion ensued about the two Alma Maters. They bickered over curriculum, campus structure, student government, et cetera, but the real conversation, the underlying jab, was about the competence of historically black universities versus white universities.

Kevin, Martin's friend and fellow alumnus met up with them about an hour into the discussion. He sat down and loosened his tie, listening to the back and forth, and shook his head. It was the same ole thing. It seemed that every time he and Martin went out with White boys, they always wanted to talk about who is better. Inadvertently and undercover, for sure. But it was always the same discussion. Don't they ever get tired of it?

While he sipped on a Kahlua and Cream, the old white magic went to work. His friends called it white magic because Kevin had a knack for picking up women without even trying to. White women. He was like a magnet. They flocked to him like he was the best thing since hot cakes. The first one that came over was blonde. She was tall and slender with breasts as big and round as the water balloons that kids used to throw off the roof to hit the mailman. Martin had a fleeting daydream about touching them. He wondered if they would pop if he squeezed too hard. He chuckled at the mental image and caught a glimpse at Jeremy and his friends. Jeremy was looking distractedly around the table and the bar. It was so deliberate, the way he looked past Kevin and the girl. He looked as if he wished that no one could see him sitting there. He creatively dodged the courting going on in front of him, if that's what you called it, by pretending to be intensely interested in the busy crowd funneling into the tiny bar. He watched as men checked women out and women coyly lured men in with no interest. He just needed something to avert his eyes from the scene unraveling before him. Brad had a sour look on his face. He kept staring at the girl, trying desperately to make eye contact. Chuck looked like he was going to be sick. His skin had taken on a strange green tone and his eyes were watery. The murmur of the crowd around them seemed far away.

Martin looked at Kevin and his lady du jour. He was working it, throwing every line he could at her. She was sitting on the stool closest to him. So close she could probably feel his breath on her face. She was fine. Martin was sure that's why Jeremy and his friends were reacting the way they were. Jealousy, pure and simple. He applauded Kevin inside.

Kevin got the girl's number and kissed her lightly before she left. When she walked away, he shot Martin a look that said, 'No sweat, man. It's as easy as pie.' Martin shook his head and laughed as he patted him on the back. That was his boy. Martin never had a problem getting girls either. He had been told time and time again that his soft hazel brown eyes were capable of hypnotizing women. That's what they said after the fact. Martin hadn't figured out the trick to make women come after *him*. Sure, he could close the deal when he went to them, but they hardly ever made that uncertain, 'everyone's looking at me' walk across a crowded room to go and talk to him like they did for Kevin. None of them. Black, White, Asian, Spanish, Indian, none of them. Not for Martin.

Kevin had to work at getting play with his own, though. Black women were used to his chocolate brown skin being silky-smooth. They were used to his naturally curly hair having a little wave to it. Black women didn't bug out on that kind of stuff. It didn't float them as easily as it floated White women. White women just loved Kevin's 'deep' skin. It was enough to make a light-skinned brother like Martin mad. Not that he wanted attention from White women so much; he was quite content with his Black Queens. But it was an ego thing. Play seemed to fall into Kevin's lap and Martin had to work for his. That kind of thing messes with a man's head.

The six of them started talking again. The conversation seemed so normal, and everyone seemed to be having such a good time that Martin shook off what he thought he saw when Kevin was talking to the woman. Not ten minutes after the blonde-haired woman left did a brown-haired woman stare in Kevin's direction. He saw her and motioned for her to come over to the table. White magic. Kevin was player-elite again. Just like that.

As Kevin turned his back to the guys, Martin got ready to comment on his 'flow' in jest. But he didn't. When he looked at Jeremy and his friends, their expressions were indescribable. There was an evil look mirrored on all four of their faces. Mutual disgust. It was only there for a second, just one split second, but Martin saw it. He saw it, and it made him uneasy. It made him angry. That was the last time they all hung out.

But there, in the lunch area at work, Martin couldn't ignore the challenge. Even though he didn't particularly care for Jeremy and his friends, he couldn't make himself pass it up. He knew that he and his boys could beat any bunch of White men at any sport, except maybe hockey. He knew that like he knew his own name. He relished the idea of being able to beat Jeremy and his boys at their own game. Martin wanted to beat them for the look they gave Kevin at the bar, or at least, the look he *thought* they gave Kevin. He had never told anyone about that because he wasn't one hundred percent sure he saw it. He had been drinking, after all. He wanted to beat them for what that look really meant.

Martin got himself so riled up that he fantasized about the game. The night before the event, Martin, Kevin, Shaun, Gary, Craig, and Robert went out for drinks. After about three beers and a lot of trash talking Martin slipped into an alcohol-induced daydream. He envisioned a plantation on which he and his friends were slaves. They had been taken from Africa to work for Jeremy and his kind. Martin imagined a great uprising where he and his friends broke their shackles and ran for the woods, determined to gain their freedom. The slave owners, led by Jeremy, advanced upon them with fire lighting their way, but he and his friends fought them off and made them retreat. Chuckling himself back to reality, Martin raised his fourth beer in a toast.

"Let's show Jeremy and his boys who's runnin' shit up in here. Paintball, basketball, baseball, racquetball, any kind of ball game they want. There's no stoppin' us."

They all raised their bottles and toasted declaration. They were ready for paintball.

That was the last time they drank together.

2

"Man, I don't think we're going the right way," Shaun muttered as they passed through the farmland. It was a gray and cool day. Something about how the sky looked bothered him. He wasn't up for this, not like the others were. He glanced warily out of the window.

"Look, Martin. There's a sign." Craig pointed at a little card stock sign flopping around on its stick. It was colored with what must have been fluorescent paint a long time ago. Now it just looked like faded orange and yellow.

'Pete's Paintball.
Play with a group.
Next Left.'

"I'm guessing that's it," Craig said playfully.

"No shit, Sherlock," Martin retorted. He made a left turn into a makeshift driveway.

There had been a lot of rain in the area over the past couple of days and the land was nothing but a muddy mess. Martin drove slowly, being careful not to get stuck. He didn't know how far the paintball field was from where they were, which was out in the middle of nowhere. It was certainly not the right time to get stuck, if there ever was a right time. Gary pulled off the driveway and onto the grass. The Jetta couldn't handle the mud. Martin decided to do the same and he followed Gary up a winding driveway that led onto a private street.

In the overcast lighting of the Saturday morning, the tree-lined street looked ominous. There were towering oak and maple trees growing haphazardly in the thick of the woods. The leaves had been falling for the past couple of weeks and the ground was covered with what looked like two inches of red and orange foliage. Evergreens and cedar trees stood tall and thick. They were sinister-looking on that cold November day. The trees were unyielding. Their appearance was upstaged by the leafless, contorted branches of the dogwood and magnolia trees that lurked in the thick. They deflected one's sight from the pine trees and the tangled brush. The trunks looked like horribly distorted torsos in the light of that overcast day. They likened themselves to a visual of tortured souls. The branches seemed to be reaching towards the cars, trying to suck them into the thick underbrush that lay below their massive bases. Shaun recoiled in his seat at the sight of them.

"Y'all ready to kick some ass?" Martin shouted in the truck. He was trying to rile them up; trying to get them motivated for the excursion. He too felt a little funny about the woods they were driving deeper into. He didn't like the sight of it one bit. But what the hell? It was just a stupid paintball game for kids. Right?

"Yeah, man. Yeah! I can feel the gun in my hands already." Craig held an imaginary gun in the shape of a rifle and aimed out of the window. With one eye squeezed shut, he cocked it and shot. He looked out at the trees. It seemed like the leaves rustled just as he shot the fake plug into the woods. He shivered unconsciously.

3

He saw a Cherokee and a Jetta make the turn onto the road leading to the paintball site through his binoculars. He zoomed in and saw one of the boys in the car looking around his woods nervously. He chuckled to himself. 'Be nervous, boy. Should be. Ain't got no kinda idea what you got comin' do ya? Soon enough, though. Soon enough,' the old man said to the empty room and let out a cackling laugh that shook his entire body. He put down the binoculars and called to his son.

4

M artin jumped out of the truck onto the moist, leaf-covered ground and looked around slowly. He tossed his keys back to Craig, like usual. Martin had been prone to losing his keys. Since he was eighteen or so he had passed his keys to Craig for safekeeping. Craig picked on him when he did it. He would make a big deal about it, laughing and calling him absent-minded. This time he didn't say a word.

It was quiet. He could hear the leaves crunching under his feet as he walked. Tall, threatening trees stood around them, encasing them in a wooden heaven... or hell. Shaun was the first one to break the silence.

"I don't think I've ever been out in woods like these. I mean, my grandmother's house has a little patch of trees in the back, but nothing like this. It's so..."

"Dark," Gary cut in. He put the steering wheel lock

on his Jetta out of habit and got out of the car. His face looked concerned; worried. So did Kevin's.

"Hey y'all! C'mon back this way. The paintball field is way in the back, down here." A short man came out from behind the bushes and called out to them. It was like he came out of nowhere. He was wearing dingy overalls and an old baseball cap that had seen better days. With a grin, he motioned for them to follow him deeper into the woods on foot. Martin went first. He thought that if he didn't no one would. As he followed the old man and heard his friends falling in behind him, he thought about the last five minutes. They got out of the car in what seemed like a barren patch of land in the woods. There was no sound. There was no movement other than their own. Suddenly there was a guy talking at them. Giddy like. It looked as though he was excited to see them. Exceedingly excited. Something was wrong with that. Martin was uneasy, but he didn't want to let his friends know that. They already seemed a little apprehensive about the situation. He walked behind the old man with caution.

They went down a steep hill that led deeper into the woods. Robert looked back and couldn't see the car. He whispered to Martin, "I can't even see the car anymore. We're really going deep in here, huh?"

"Good," Martin said without turning around, "This way we won't hit the cars with any paint. You know I'd be pissed off if I messed up my truck."

He chuckled and picked up the pace behind the man. Robert looked back towards the car and shook his head, disturbed.

The man stopped in front of a dilapidated wooden shed and said, "Right here's where y'all will meet up wit' the other team. Go'n be a good game today, yup. Imma go an' get 'em right now. Y'all stay put." He walked around the corner and disappeared as quickly as he had appeared by the cars. They and looked at each other in silence. Kevin said, "So, what do we do now," Gary asked.

"I guess we wait. Jeremy will be here soon enough," Martin said. After about 15 minutes Martin saw them coming down the hill, eight strong. They were dressed in fatigues and seemed in unison with their stride. Looking at them was like watching a platoon prepare for battle. They were focused and serious. Martin's stomach dropped.

Jeremy was ahead of the pack. He looked confident and determined. He walked up to Martin and said with a straight face, "I'm really glad you came. You and your...friends."

He glanced through them, committing their innuendoes to memory. He looked back at Martin with soft venom in his eyes. Martin saw the change in Jeremy, but only for a second. He wasn't sure what it meant but he didn't like it. He was starting not to like much about the set up for this game.

Jeremy's face lightened and he offered a chuckle, but his eyes remained cold. He said, "You remember Chuck, Kurt, and Brad, don't you? Eddie, Doug, Wally, and Steve came along too. This should be a real good game."

"You've met Kevin. This is Shaun, Gary, Craig, and

Robert." Martin pointed them out one by one to Jeremy and his friends. It was a stare down, but no one acknowledged it as such. It became clear to Martin that they weren't there just to play tag in the woods. "Looks like we've got two more guys than you do. Tell you what, why don't we even it up? Make it seven on seven. Take your pick of one of our men," Jeremy said to Martin. He was smiling, but there was no warmth coming from it. He was cold. There was something glistening maliciously in his eyes. Hate, fear, jealousy, Martin wasn't sure. But he saw it... again. And Jeremy knew it.

Martin looked at the guys Jeremy brought with him. They were all of average build, nothing spectacular. *'Nothing me and my boys can't handle,'* the little voice in his head chimed in. They all had a certain confidence about them. Not inherent, he didn't think. No, it was more like they had set something up, some prime situation that they had complete control over. They were ready to play. They were sure to win. He glanced tentatively at his friends. They were all strong, all athletic. Physically, Jeremy and his friends were no match for them. But something in the back of his mind told him that this was not going to be a challenge of will and stamina. This would be something worse than that... something much more important than that.

Craig spoke up and said, "OK, since we get to pick. How about you?"

Craig pointed at Chuck. He was the bulkiest guy on Jeremy's team. He looked like he worked out more than the others, and that would make him able to handle the challenge ahead. He thought.

"What's your name, partner?"

"Chuck," he said as he snickered and looked back at his friends. He walked towards Martin's team and said, "Sure, I'm game."

"Looks like we've got a game, then! Let's head up so we can get this started," Jeremy announced as he led the way to the ammo station. They followed in single file, silently, contemplating the situation. Shaun looked over at Martin as if to ask a question but shook his head instead. Martin shrugged and slapped Shaun on the back in an effort to reassure him that things were cool. It was just a game, after all. Shaun looked away; his face grimaced slightly with worry.

5

Both teams got their ammo and bought extra just in case they ran out in the heat of battle. While they loaded their guns, Martin and his team had a strategy huddle. "We have to be ready for them to come out of a bag on us. Jeremy knows this is our first time playing. We're not going to let them take us though, right?" he questioned.

"Naw man, no. This'll be a piece of cake. We just have to stick to the plan. Get the flag and cover each other," Kevin offered.

"We should make sure that we have one person at the fort protecting the flag at all times, just in case they infiltrate somehow," Chuck added.

"Yeah, yeah. I don't know about you, but I want to be out in the middle of things. I want to go for the flag and bring it home," Robert said uncharacteristically. Robert was usually the one who waited for other people to take control of things before he jumped in. He'd been that way for as long as Martin had known him, and that was about 10 years. In high school he wouldn't go out for basketball unless at least one of his boys was going out for it too. He wouldn't go to a party unless one of his boys was going, even when a girl asked him to go. He even went to Howard University because Martin and Kevin were going. So, when he stepped up to the plate, wanting to be the one to go for the flag, everyone looked at him in shock.

Robert looked at their surprised eyes and said, "What? A brother can't want his 15 minutes of fame? Step off, y'all."

They laughed as he rolled his eyes. Shaun looked over at the other group while his laughter subsided. They weren't in a huddle like his team was, strategizing and planning. They weren't talking to each other at all. Jeremy and his team were staring at them. One of them was looking right into his eyes. Shaun looked back, unwilling to tear his eyes away. Unwilling or unable. Everything else became dark around him. Tunnel vision blocked everyone else out. The shirt the guy was wearing was completely out of focus and the features of his face were blurry. The only things Shaun could see clearly were his eyes. They were a light shade of green, but to Shaun, they looked as black as ebony. Dark and small. They were so hot they could bore holes into his head, he thought. He looked away to shake himself from the grip.

"You OK, man?" Craig asked him. He looked like he had just seen a ghost. Craig looked in the direction that Shaun had been staring and saw nothing out of the ordinary. Just the other team going over their plans, just like they had been doing. He put his hand on Shaun's back and said, "Man, what's the deal?"

"I don't know, I thought I saw something. I thought-" He stopped short and looked at Chuck. He was staring at him with dark eyes...for one second. When he blinked Chuck looked normal. He looked like a regular guy, concerned for his teammate. Not like a ghoul or a man with something up his sleeve. Just a regular guy.

"Nothing. I'm cool. I'm cool," Shaun said. He glanced tentatively back at Chuck who still looked … normal. A shiver crept up his spine.

"OK, since Robert's layin' down the law, we go with that plan," Kevin continued. "Me and Rob'll go up the middle for the flag. We'll need two to stay with our flag and everyone else needs to disperse and take care of things as they come. Sound like a plan?"

"Yeah, that'll work," Shaun offered. He sounded more like he was trying to convince himself than just agreeing with the plan.

They broke the huddle and prepared for the referee's word. A beefy man dressed in fatigues with a fluorescent orange pull over vest stretched tightly across his torso stood between the two teams. Martin looked at him and nodded hello. The man returned a smirk and glanced over to Jeremy's team with a knowing glance. Confused, Martin looked at Kevin who was standing next to him, and said, "Did you see that Ref? What's up with that?"

"I don't know, man," he said as he looked at Jeremy

and his friends. They were ready. Mentally and physically. They had all the extras also. They had smoke bombs, side arms, grenades, you name it. He didn't even know they made those kinds of accessories for paintball. Something about that made him nervous. Martin shook his head lightly. "Don't sweat it," he finished.

The referee spoke loudly into the bullhorn. In a muffled voice he yelled, "The idea is to get the flag and take it to your fort. If you get hit three times, you out the game fer good. Do y'all get that? The game is over when one team has taken the other team's flag, or when there's only one man standing. Got that? Play to the end, boys. This is war." He held up two bandannas – one yellow and one red. "These is yo' flags. Jeremy's boys got the yellow one and you boys got the red one." He tossed the flag lackadaisically to Martin. "If there ain't no questions, I say let's get this goin'. Any questions?" No one said anything.

"When I blow this whistle, it means y'all got 'bout one minute to get to yo' places. When I blow it again the game starts. Here she goes."

He licked the perspiration off his upper lip and blew into the whistle. The two teams dispersed, hanging their flags in equi-distant forts on low branches, and securing their hiding places. They moved without a sound. Martin and Shaun were protecting the flag, Robert and Kevin were the flag runners going up the middle on opposite sides of the path, and Craig, Chuck and Gary were on the outskirts protecting the flag runners like line backers.

When Kevin got to his hiding place, he could hear Shaun behind him breathing heavily.

"What is it, man? You ok?"

"Yeah man. I-I'm fine," Shaun responded. But he was far from fine.

The whistle sounded for the second time.

The game had begun.

6

They sat in complete silence for an eternity. Their hearts beat loudly and rapidly in their chests. Martin looked between the bushes at his friends. They were tense and uptight. There was something brewing in the woods that was more than competitiveness. It was more like fear. Genuine, uncontested fear. And they all felt it. Even him.

Kevin knelt hidden in the brush, covered by leaves and twigs as camouflage. Beads of sweat fell into his eyes underneath the protective goggles, stinging them, but he dared not wipe his forehead. He didn't want to move at all. Something was going on and he knew it. *'Something is wrong with this set up,'* he thought. *'I mean, those guys came down looking serious about...something.'* This wasn't just an ordinary game of paintball. He knew it the moment he saw the other team. He could tell by the way Jeremy and his friends were looking at them. Jeremy and his friends were looking at them like they were fresh meat, a succulent cut at that. It made him nervous.

He looked beyond the tree at Jeremy's fort. He could barely see their flag above the bushes and tall grass. He couldn't see any of Jeremy's team either. Not one person. He adjusted his footing and raised up slightly to get a better look. He thought he saw movement, so he shot off a round of pink paint. The paintball shot out of the gun propelled by the CO_2 tank connected to its base and splattered against a tree. When there was no retaliation, Kevin relaxed back into his hiding place. He didn't see the gunman in the bushes picking him out. He didn't hear the barrel cock as the gunman took aim. He didn't see the barrel squared off at his head. He didn't hear the bullet cut the air. He didn't see or hear anything at all.

"Did you hear that," Shaun shrieked in a low, raspy, panicked voice. They all hit the dirt as soon as the pop of the bullet broke the uncomfortable silence. "It sounded like gun fire. Real gunfire, man! What the fuck is going on?"

Martin was crouched in the thick of kikuyu grass, his eyes searching frantically. The shot rang in his ears loudly, incessantly. He looked nervously around for his friends. Robert was standing now, looking around himself in fear. Martin wanted to yell out to Robert and tell him to sit down, to take cover, to run damnit, but when he opened his mouth, nothing came out. Nothing. He tried to inch towards Shaun who was across the weathered path from him, lying in a makeshift bunker. He wanted to go to him so that he wouldn't be alone. So that neither one of them would be alone... but he couldn't move.

A second shot was fired, and a gargled scream

permeated the air thick with tension and fear. Martin looked up just in time to see Robert grab at his throat. Blood shot out in spurts between his fingers, mimicking his racing heartbeat. Robert gagged and coughed, trying desperately to catch his breath. His bulging eyes were glazed over with pain. He fell to his knees and sprayed the mallow with his dying blood.

'Oh Shit! Oh, Holy shit,' Martin thought to himself. He peered over the tangle weed he had buried himself under and saw Chuck retracting into his hiding place. Chuck! The big guy on *their* team, courtesy of Jeremy. *'He led them right to us,'* Martin thought fleetingly. Chuck had a hideous smirk on his face. He was laughing. They were all laughing. The low roar of their impervious glee seared his eardrums.

"Got that, boys? We fixin' to play us a good ole game of paintball today," someone shouted into the thick air. It was Jeremy's voice.

"Yeah, your blood will do nicely in place of paint. Those balls don't quite splatter the way blood does, you know. It's just not the same. So we go'n make sure we do this right. Why, we wouldn't want to bring you all the way out here to play a half-assed game. We want to make sure your first game of paintball is the real thing. Your first and your last, that is." He heard Jeremy chuckle and walk away. The crunching of the leaves under his feet became distant, and it sounded like he was walking back towards the common ground. Jeremy might have left, but the others hadn't moved. They were laying in wait, ready to pounce. Waiting…

8

He could hear the laughter emanating from the bushes. He could hear the distant gait of Jeremy's smooth, calm step. He could hear his heart thumping wildly in his chest; he could hear all of these things. He could also hear, underneath all of the peripheral noise, he could hear Shaun panting heavily, trying desperately to get a handle on himself and the situation. He could hear Craig shaking against the dead leaves. He could hear Gary's soft cries of confusion. Martin heard it all. He covered his ears and sank his head. A deep, guttural yell rose from his diaphragm, shaking his body in anger and dread.

It seemed like hours before he moved. He could see Martin's shoulders heaving massively as he sobbed loudly. God, he wanted to get up and run. He wanted to run for his life. Instead, all he could do was stare at Martin's back as hot tears streamed down his face.

"Shaun? Shaun??" He heard his name whispered in the cool of the unfolding day and it woke him from the trance he slipped into.

"Shaun," Gary pled.

"Yeah man, yeah. I'm here, man."

Gary inched close to the ground trying not to make a sound. He crawled over to Martin first and put his arm around him. Martin hadn't moved. His mouth was still open, shaped in the grimace left from his painful shout. Tears had dried on his cheeks and he dry-heaved sporadically and rapidly. Gary made his way through the fallen leaves to Shaun and said,

"D-D-Did that sh-sh-shit really ha-p-p-p-pen, man? Did you see that sh-sh-shit-t?"

Shaun looked at him vapidly and nodded. Gary was stammering badly. In the seventeen years that they had known each other, Shaun hadn't heard Gary stammer or stutter or trip once.

Not once.

He grabbed Gary by the shoulders as he shook and said, "I saw it man. Good God, I saw Robert go down."

"Where is everybody? Where are they man? Kevin? Craig? Where-"

"Kevin's dead, G. Kevin's gone, man," Craig said from behind them. Martin looked up slowly from the ball he had rolled his body into. His eyes searched Craig's face, laden with mud and leaves and blood. There was blood on his jacket; it glistened in the dull light that the trees let through.

"Are you hit, C.? You alright, man," Gary asked him in a shaky, high-pitched tenor, far from his usual baritone rumble.

Craig looked down at his jacket and said,

"No, it's not my blood. I'm not hit. I was next to Kevin when he went down. I guess I wasn't as far out on the perimeter as I was supposed to be. The shot was so loud, I thought I would never stop hearing the echo. They came from somewhere behind us. They were hiding in the bushes, but there's no way they could have gotten to that position so quick. It was like he got shot seconds after the game started. It wasn't even a minute after the second whistle blew before they gunned him down."

They looked at each other in silence. Craig touched the blood on his jacket and began to sob.

"Where are they now," the old man asked Jeremy. He looked pleased but on guard. He paced the room, his toeless foot thumping on the floor hard in unison with his wooden cane with each step. A glaze of sweat was forming on his forehead. He laughed heartily before Jeremy could answer and shook his fist towards the window in defiance.

"Who says we don't own this land, huh," he shouted. "Them niggers think they runnin' us - they think they runnin' everything! They think they such hot shit. We showin' them different, ain't we boys? We finally putting them in they fuckin' places, yup. This is where they belong. In the jungle running scared like animals and hiding like cowards and then dying at the hand of a righteous man. A White man. It's how it always should have been, and would have, if it hadn't been for those bleeding heart bastards and uppity niggers like King and Evers. Fuckin' coons. Too weak to be a buck so they got book smart. But that book smart shit don't work out here in our place, do it boys? These fuckin' coon bastards go'n suffer today. And pretty soon our mission will take out all of 'em. All of 'em!"

He raised his hands in the air in triumph and Jeremy's hands raised to meet them. "There are four left, Dad. We shot two of those fuckers down already. One of 'em spurted his blood all over the leaves out there. Big fuckin' mess."

"Don't worry about it, boy. Nigger blood is better than rain."

Jeremy smiled and patted his dad on the back. He turned to the door and walked into the hallway. He stuck his head out and said, "Eddie, you ready for part two?"

"Jerry, I don't think we even have to do it. They're easy pickins out there. They ain't got shit for bullets and we got them outnumbered."

"I know, but it'll be that much sweeter to see them fall for our trick. Trust me on this one. You'll see."

The four of them sat together in a huddle. The wind was whipping up and the air was getting cold. How long had they been out there? An hour, maybe two? In that short time their lives had changed forever.

In the bushes to their front right they could hear bugs chirping and buzzing loudly over Robert's body. The hot, pungent smell of fresh blood saturated the air and made it hard to breathe. It was their friends' blood. Robert's and Kevin's.

Craig spoke first, "Look, we don't have anything but paintballs in here. No bullets. We are sitting ducks if we don't run for it. There's no other way." He looked into the clear plastic cover and saw fluorescent pink and yellow paint balls in the hopper. He shook his head. "We've got to go for it."

"What and give them free target practice?" Shaun exclaimed. His face was covered with sweat and tears.

His lips quivered as he spoke, "We can't just run out there and book to the cars hoping to hell none of us gets our asses blown off! Who knows where they are now, just waiting for us to make a fool move like that so they can cut us down?"

"He's right," Martin said. He had been silent since Robert's death, unable to speak, unable to think. "We can't just *run* out of here. We need a plan."

They put their heads together to come up with a way out. Splitting up was the only option. They dumped their worthless guns and facemasks and moved within the bushes as quietly as possible, veering off gradually in different directions. The plan was to get to the cars and wait for each other. The first ones to the car were supposed to hide on the floor until all four of them got in. They were going to put the cars in neutral and let it roll down the incline they were parked on. When the cars rolled far enough away from the woods, they would start the engines and Jeremy and his friends would have to run to catch them. They could escape if they stuck to the plan. They could get out.

12

They moved with very little sound and found themselves alone quickly. Shaun crouched and crawled through prickly tangle weed, wincing from the pain, but not uttering a sound. Then he heard something. He kept going; afraid to stop now…and then he heard it again. A low, jumbled sound was coming from the bushes off to his right. It sounded like moaning. His mind flooded with thoughts of Kevin or Robert lying in the cold mud, colored red by their blood. He thought of one of them gasping for air and mouthing his or one of the other guy's names, begging for help.

He whispered, "Kevin? Kevin man, that you?"

It had to be Kevin if it was anyone at all. He saw Robert get shot with his own eyes. He saw the blood and the distant look in his eyes before he was engulfed by the bushes. He knew Robert couldn't be alive.

No answer. Maybe the wind was playing tricks on him. Maybe he wanted it to be one of his friends so badly that he made himself believe they were calling to him. Maybe… A voice beckoned weakly from the bushes. He moved closer, no longer cognizant of the noise he was making.

"Kevin? You're alive?"

He pulled back a branch and uncovered Eddie, one of Jeremy's friends. He was bleeding from a shot to his left shoulder. His gun was lying on the ground close to his right foot, and his shirt was ripped to shreds. He was propped unsteadily on the menacing tree stump, his back painfully hunched.

Shaun recoiled quickly and started to run. He could almost feel the beam of the gun on his back, targeting his heart through his clothes. He was terrified.

Eddie wheezed, "No! Please help me."

Shaun stopped running and turned his head towards Eddie cautiously. Eddie was injured, the pain on his face was unmistakable. He was reaching for Shaun earnestly, wanting-- needing help.

Shaun stood in place and said, "You didn't see me, man. Keep it that way." He turned to leave, but Eddie whispered, "SHH! Be quiet. They're all around here. They're waiting for you - for us."

Shaun looked around him and saw nothing but the twisted branches of trees and evergreen shrubs. He listened intently and heard nothing but the birds vacating the area, in search of warmer weather. Getting away. Like he wanted to.

Shaun walked towards Eddie. "What do you mean *us*? You're one of *them*. Why would they be looking for you?" He nudged Eddie's gun away from him and brought it to his side. Eddie let him do it.

"See man? I'm safe. I'm not with what the other guys are doing." He sucked in air heavily and with marked difficulty. There was blood all over him. It saturated his shirt. He was sweating profusely and shaking slightly. Shaun didn't hold the gun on him, but he kept it close to his side.

"I'm not with them, I swear it. I don't know what's going on. I've known Jeremy for years-- ever since we were kids...I don't know what's happening." He breathed in thickly again and coughed. He trembled violently and turned red.

Shaun watched him convulse. He wanted to believe him, but he had to be sure.

"That's bullshit. How could you not know what 's going on? You're one of them! You're on their team! You planned this with them from the start!"

"No, no. I swear, I didn't have any idea this was going to happen. I came out here from Boston to see Jeremy on Friday. He told me he was going to be playing paintball with a couple of friends and a colleague from work. A friendly game, that's all. I never knew there was going to be anything like this. Dear God, if I had known... do you honestly think I would be in this situation if I knew?"

He shifted his weight and gestured towards his wound.

Shaun sighed, "Why'd they do that to you man? Why'd they shoot you and how did you stop them from killing you?"

"Jeremy -" He stifled a sob. "Jeremy shot me. After he shot the first one, your friend, I asked him what the hell was going on. I thought we were just going to play paintball. I had no idea anything like this was going to happen. I told him I wouldn't be involved in this and that I was going to find you guys and help you get out. I told him that what he was doing wasn't right. That it just wasn't right. He…he shot me with absolutely no remorse. He left me to die. He said that he wanted me to suffer, and that he hoped that one of you guys found me and beat me to death. I crawled down here from up the hill. I was trying to get help, but I…I'm so tired. God man, we've been friends for so long I can't believe…I can't believe what he's doing."

Eddie turned his head away from Shaun and sniffled. He pulled his arm up to his eyes and buried his head in it. Shaun watched him as he went through his pain. He had just lost two of his closest friends, so he understood what Eddie was going through. Eddie's body began to shake. Shaun put his hand on Eddie's shoulder to comfort him. He propped the gun against a tree and covered his own eyes as he let his emotion out.

Eddie continued to cry as he quickly put his hand, clad with open handcuffs that were hidden in the bushes, on Shaun's right wrist. Shaun looked up in surprise. The realization that he had been fooled came over him. Before he could process this betrayal - before he could react at all, the hand that held the tears he shed for his lost friends was locked viciously in the cold iron cuff. Shaun couldn't believe what was happening.

Eddie's cries of pain and anguish turned into hearty laughter.

He stood and exclaimed, "Whoa, Jerry! You were right! That trick sure as hell did work!"

Eddie leaned down and whispered into Shaun's ear. "Your nigger friend's blood was still warm when I took some and smeared it on my shirt."

Shaun yelled out loud in fear and anger.

Eddie continued to laugh as Jeremy came from behind a nearby bush. He smiled at Eddie, pleased with his work. "Take 'im back to the shed, Eddie. We'll set up the rest of it. Oh, and gag 'im so he cain't shout."

Eddie nodded and giggled as he led dumbfounded Shaun to the shed. Jeremy shouted at the top of his lungs,

" Boys, we got one of yo' nigger friends now. If you want his tired ass, you'll come get 'im at the shed. If all of you ain't there in, oh say 15 minutes, we'll kill 'im and skin 'im. Ain't that what happened to that stupid nigger Nat Turner?" He chuckled and said, "You niggers are just as dumb and gullible as they say you are. This shit is easy as taking candy from a baby."

He strolled towards the shed, shooting the blanks out of Eddie's gun into the air.

13

Martin stopped in his tracks and looked around as Jeremy beckoned for them to come to the shed. They caught someone. Who? How? He sat on the ground and looked at his hands. He didn't know what to do. He knew he had to find the others if they were still in the woods...if they were still alive.

Craig turned around quickly at the end of Jeremy's diatribe. The woods seemed to be closing in on him. The trees seemed to be laughing at him. He suddenly felt very small. The claustrophobia that he had once overcome came back viciously and overtook him. He fell to the ground wide-eyed and unable to breathe sufficiently. He was paralyzed by fear.

ary ran down the hill and out of the consuming wilderness, ignoring Jeremy's call to the shed. He could see the cars up ahead. He was so close; he could almost touch them. He kept running, not once looking back, not even when Jeremy reiterated that he had captured one of his friends, not even when he heard the gunfire. With tears in his eyes, he ran to the Jetta. He fumbled with the keys in his pocket, having trouble grabbing them and pulling them out because his hands were shaking so badly.

There were footsteps behind him. They were rapidly approaching. He could hear the heavy breathing and the wheezing, shaky voice uttering what sounded like his name. Elated, he turned around thinking that one of his friends made it out. With a smile he extended his arms, only to see that it was Brad, one of Jeremy's boys. He was holding a double-barrel rifle at his chest. Brad was so close, Gary could feel the edge of the barrel grazing the button on the pocket of his shirt.

"C'mon man. Let me go. You don't have to kill me, OK? You don't have to do this, man."

Brad looked at him gravely, not moving a muscle in his face. With a placid, strong voice he said, "Yes, I do."

He pulled the trigger.

14

Martin clawed through the bushes to find his way back to their fort. With no other safe, as if any place was really *safe*, common ground, he hoped that the others would think to meet there after hearing the announcement.

Martin got to the clearing and fell clumsily to the ground, his body wracked with exhaustion and fear. Frantically he tried to think of who could have been caught. Shaun? Gary? Craig? He didn't know. He tried to be quiet and wait for the others, but his mind was throwing all different kinds of scenarios at him. Could Jeremy have been bluffing and this was a set up? Did Jeremy really have one of them and, if he did, was he still alive? Martin didn't know. He couldn't believe any of this was happening. It seemed like a dream. One that he couldn't wake himself from. It was a horrid nightmare.

Craig came around the corner huffing and puffing. "Where are the others?"

"I don't know. What took you so long to get back?"

"I was out of it, man. The trees, they looked like they were closing in on me. I guess I slipped back into one of those fits I used to have when I was a kid. You know, the ones where I can't move at all, no matter what I do. I snapped out of it a couple of minutes after the gunfire. When I was running back here, I thought I heard more gunfire but it was off in the distance. Did you hear it?"

Martin nodded solemnly. He heard the shot but hadn't processed it until Craig brought it up. *'My God, did one of us get shot,'* he though.

"Who do you suppose they have? Gary or Shaun?" Craig continued.

"I don't know, but we only have seven minutes or so to get to that shed they were talking about. I hope whoever's left, Shaun or Gary, will go right to the shed. We can't afford to waste anymore time waiting for them."

Martin got up and started to walk into the bushes toward the shed, or in that general direction. Reluctantly, Craig followed behind him, looking back every now and then to see if either Shaun or Gary showed up at their fort. Both Martin and Craig had lost their sense of direction with all the running in circles, and they couldn't recall where the shed was.

They made their way to Jeremy's fort and beyond, still not seeing any sign of the shed. Frustrated and scared with only three minutes left, Martin turned his head up to the sky and shouted, "Where are you, Jeremy? What the hell do you want from us?"

He threw his arms out to his sides in rage. A sarcastic chuckle came from behind them. Slowly Jeremy emerged from the woods. It looked almost like he was arriving from another dimension, the way he seemed to glide out and away from the bushes and trees, floating towards them with unnatural grace. He was unarmed and stripped of the bulky garments they had all worn to keep warm during the game. He was sweating bullets, as though he had been running through the woods, tracking their steps. He was smiling demonically, pleased with the cat and mouse game he had set up.

Hatred welled in Martin's throat, suffocating his rational thoughts. He lunged at Jeremy, throwing all of his weight at him. Jeremy leaned to the side and tripped Martin. He fell flat on his face. Martin turned over onto his back and looked up at him. Jeremy was *smiling*. Craig went over to Martin and helped him to his feet.

"You 'bout done now? I can stand here and fight you 'till the cows come home, but your friend is going to run out of time. Tick, tock. Tick, tock. The seconds keep a' tickin' away." He turned towards the bushes and started to walk away.

The southern drawl Jeremy was displaying was new to Martin. He had never heard it before that day. He didn't think he would ever forget it. Craig nudged him along and they followed Jeremy into the woods.

Jeremy had a streak of blood down the back of his grimy tee-shirt. It was thick and wide with bits and pieces of flesh on it. Craig gagged as they walked, unable to fathom whose blood that might be. He stumbled and tripped over his feet, falling to the ground. He was feeling the same feeling that plagued him before. The trees were starting to close in on him. They mocked him with intangible laughter and pointed their accusatory fingers at him while he writhed on the floor, gasping for air, precious air.

Martin went to him and raised him to a sitting position. Jeremy was drifting out of sight.

"C'mon, C. Get up, man. We've got to go and save our boy. Please Craig. I don't even see Jeremy anymore. We've got to catch up to him."

Craig tried desperately to catch his breath, but he couldn't. He tried to wave Martin on, but his limbs were heavy. His face turned ashy gray from the lack of oxygen, and he started to fade. Faintly now, he could hear Martin begging him not to die. Telling him to hold on. He could see out of the corner of his eye something - someone laying on the ground next to him, hidden away from sight under the bushes. It was Gary. His eyes were upturned, and his face had a tormented grimace forever etched on it. Without fighting he allowed himself to slip into unconsciousness. He couldn't take any more of what was happening.

15

Martin watched his friend drift off helplessly. He couldn't stay with him. It was already too late. Jeremy had completely disappeared in the brush, and Martin only had one minute left to help his friend. He got up slowly, saying a silent goodbye, and ran in the direction Jeremy was headed, casting a solemn look back at his friend Craig who lay partially under the bushes.

Martin caught up to Jeremy quickly and said, "How far are we from it, man?"

"Is that nigger friend of yours dead," Jeremy asked maliciously with his back still turned.

"Yes. He is."

"Bonus. That way I don't have to waste a round on him."

"Is that your plan? To kill us all?" Martin's voice had taken on a shrill quality. It was the sound of panic and disarmament.

Jeremy stopped walking and stood with his back to Martin. He pondered the question for a moment. Suddenly lifted his head to the sky and let out a monstrous laugh that shook Martin to his core. He shook his head and turned to look at Martin. With pity in his voice he said, "Don't you realize that you are already dead?"

He smiled and turned his back to continue deeper into the woods. He pushed the bushes away, clearing Martin's view of the shed, and of Shaun.

16

Shaun's arms and legs were bound by rope to a wooden cross that was wedged into the ground. He was completely naked. His nipples had been cut off and stuffed up his nostrils protruding them grotesquely. The jagged lacerations in his skin were bleeding profusely. Sweat covered his body and he had soiled himself. His head was lowered onto his chest. He had been beaten savagely and his skin was discolored in several places. Martin was certain that his friend was dead.

Martin saw an old man in the doorway of the shed. His eyes were gleaming. He had a look of contentment and anticipation on his face. Next to him stood Jack, the controller of the firm he and Jeremy worked for. His face was red and sweaty. It held a look of mocking satisfaction. Martin could have killed them. All of them.

Before Martin's eyes, Wally and Kurt poured gasoline on Shaun's limp body. Wally lit a match and threw it on Shaun's stomach. It stuck there while the flame ignited.

"Looks like we's fixin' ta have a right ole' Bar-B-Q, ain't we nigger," Steve said jovially. Martin was flabbergasted. Everything that he was seeing, everything he had seen was a blur to him now as he stood incoherently before his friend's burning body.

A bone-chilling scream escaped Shaun's lips and he lifted his head slowly. He shook on the makeshift cross, trying to tip it over and escape perishing in the flames. Quickly though, he was silent.

Martin snapped back to reality and attacked Kurt, pushing him into the flames with Shaun. Kurt lunged away from Shaun's burning body quickly, but he couldn't escape the flames. They clung to his face and shirt, devouring the skin underneath. He screamed deliriously in pain and threw himself on the ground. He groped for something that would extinguish the flames to no avail.

Wally threw a blanket over him and tried to beat the flames out, but it was too late.

"You muthafuckin' bitch," Steve said and grabbed Martin's arms. He threw Martin to the ground and put all of his weight on him. Martin shut his eyes; all the fight had drained out of him. He heard all too clearly the cock of the gun. He felt the cool barrel on his temple and welcomed it.

17

The gunshot woke Craig from his unconscious state. He peered through the dead leaves and roots to see if he could detect any signs of movement. He had to get out of there, he knew that now. He didn't think anyone was left from his crew. The gunshot had to be for Martin, he was sure of it. Gary was dead, Kevin was dead, Robert was dead, Shaun had to be dead. He was the only one left.

He got up and moved slowly at first, cautiously. He could hear them talking loudly and cursing about something. They sounded angry. Maybe Martin and Shaun took care of one of them before they were killed. God, he hoped they had gotten at least one of them.

Craig made his way down the hill in virtual silence, blending in with the darkening day and slipping out into oblivion. He made it to the truck and reached for Martin's keys in his pocket. They were warm against his leg. He pulled them out slowly and clenched them tightly in his hand for a moment, unable to stop the memories from flooding back. Unable to say goodbye.

Quietly he got into the truck, taking pains not to slam the door. He checked the back seats to make sure that no one was in there with him. He ducked under the windows as he slid the car into neutral. As the car rolled backwards down the incline and out of the hardened mud onto the dirt road that led to the main drag. He prayed that there was nothing behind him that he could hit and draw attention to himself. He just wanted to get out.

He felt pebbles crunching under the tires and the ride became less smooth. He was out of the mud and on some semblance of a road. He turned the ignition, shifted the truck into first gear, and took off. He kicked up rocks with the back tires as he sped down the dirt road, shifting the gears roughly and abruptly.

Craig made his way through the dense brush on either side of the road, positive that one of Jeremy's friends was waiting there for him, gun in hand, aimed and prepared, but they weren't. He made an uncontested right onto the paved road. He saw the faded paintball sign in the rear-view mirror getting smaller and smaller. Tears rolled silently down his cheeks.

Passing him quickly on his left was a red sports utility truck filled with five guys…Black guys. They made a sharp left turn into the paintball area.

THE END

THE BLACK HOLE
SCREENPLAY

The Black Hole

Written by

L. Marie Wood

FADE IN:

EXT. RURAL MARYLAND - NIGHT

The panoramic view outlines the dense and barren land
surrounding the sheriff's jailhouse. An old police cruiser,
a late model pick-up truck, and a contemporary sedan are
parked in front.

INT. SHERIFF'S DEPARTMENT - NIGHT

Four men sit in the small office area equipped with four
desks, three file cabinets, and a water cooler. The holding
cell is empty. The room is hot and humid. The four men are
perspiring.

THE OLD MAN (65), with a bad right leg; PETE (40), a wiry,
scruffy man; and JOE (47), the heavy-set officer, are
sitting in a cluster. THE FOURTH MAN, whose name is AL (30),
a slender man hidden in the shadows, paces the floor. We
SEE only The Fourth Man's back. They speak with southern
accents except The Fourth Man.

                    THE OLD MAN
              They tell me it's all set up. You
              got the field ready, Pete?

                    PETE
              Yup. Ev'rthang's ready up thar. You
              just tell me when.

                    JOE
              Make it snappy, folks. Ole Willie'll
              be in here to sleep his habit off
              soon. Y'all gotta be outta here by
              then, else this whole thang's found
              out.

                    PETE
              Ole Willie ain't go'n rememba
              nothin'! He'll be so drunk he might
              think you his bitch and try to curl
              up wit cha!

Pete hugs himself and makes a seductive face. They all
laugh except The Fourth Man.

                         JOE
              Shit, I'm prettier than his bitch!

They all laugh, except The Fourth Man.

                    THE FOURTH MAN
              You just make sure you do what you're
              supposed to, Joe.

The laughing stops abruptly. Joe looks at The Fourth Man in
a mixture of shock and annoyance. The Fourth Man faces the
window. We SEE his back.

                    THE FOURTH MAN (cont'd)
                       (continuing)
              We don't want any interruptions
              tomorrow.

Joe turns his head to The Old Man. The Old Man stares back
at Joe.

                    THE FOURTH MAN
                       (continuing)
              They'll be at the field by eleven
              o'clock. I want everything ready.
              You all better make sure of that.

We SEE The Fourth Man's silhouette, his face is shadowed.

                    THE FOURTH MAN
                       (continuing)
              I want everything to be ready for
              them.

BLACKOUT.

BEGIN TITLES

AERIAL VIEW - COUNTRY ROAD - CHEROKEE AND JETTA are driving
on the quiet road alone. Slowly PAN DOWN to the cars as
they MOVE along the road.

END TITLES

EXT. RURAL MARYLAND ROAD-ESTABLISHING SHOT- DAY

The sky is overcast and there is nothing but farmland on one side of the road and tall trees on the other. The farmland is peppered with animals grazing.

INT. CHEROKEE - DAY

Three Black men are dressed in old athletic gear. Their names are SHAUN (31), who is buff and muscular, MARTIN (29), who is of average build; and CRAIG (29), who is slender and fit - very toned. Craig and Shaun are looking out of the windows at the rural scene. Shaun rolls down the window.

> SHAUN
> Damn, man.
> (beat)
>
> Gotta bring a nigga out to the boonies to play souped up tag.

> MARTIN
> Shaun, what's up with the window?

> CRAIG
> Yeah, man. It's not like it's summer up in here.

> SHAUN
> (rolling up the window)
> Are you sure we're going the right way, Martin?

> CRAIG
> I don't see any street signs…

> SHAUN
> (elbowing Craig)
> Are you seeing this shit? It's like we drove out of Maryland and into the backwoods of North Carolina!

Shaun and Craig chuckle.

                    MARTIN
        I've followed the directions to the
        letter. They told me there wouldn't
        be any street signs. They said we
        wouldn't see anything but farmland
        for miles.

                    CRAIG
        They meant that shit, too!

They all laugh.

                    SHAUN
        Guess this is as good a place as any
        to have a paintball fight. Ain't
        nothin' to disturb out here but the
        cows…
            (points at the cows)
        … I mean, there's even a sheriff's
        department out here.

Shaun LOOKS at the sheriff's department passing on his
right.

                    SHAUN (cont'd)
            (continuing)\)
        It's like fuckin' Mayberry out here…
            (chuckling)
        … Wit'Barney Fife and shit.

                    CRAIG
        I can't believe I'm giving up my
        Saturday to come out to the sticks
        and play a kid's game with a bunch of
        White boys.

                    SHAUN
        I'm with you on that, brotha. I am
        with you on that one for real.

                    MARTIN
        Y'all talkin' like you had something
        else to do.

                    SHAUN
        I did!

                         MARTIN
              Yeah, right. Like what?
                  (beat)
              Cleanin' yo' crusty drawers?

     Martin and Craig laugh.

                         SHAUN
              No, but I could have been cleanin'
              some pretty lace panties, if you know
              what I'm sayin'.

     Martin and Craig snicker.

                         CRAIG
              Yeah, right.

                         MARTIN
              In your dreams, partner. Anyway,
              there was no way I was gonna turn
              down this challenge. You should have
              been with us in the break room
              Thursday. Jerry was kicking
              paintball to us hard. I almost had
              no choice.

     FLASHBACK - INT. BREAK ROOM IN WAREHOUSE - DAY

     Martin and KEVIN (29), a smooth and slender Black man, are
     at lunch with JERRY (32), a physically toned White man, and
     CHUCK (29) a buff, unkempt White man. The break room is
     crowded. Tables and a soda machine are the only stationary
     things in the room. The workers are both standing and
     sitting, and some are eating lunch. AD LIB chatter from the
     break room.

     INT. BREAK ROOM IN WAREHOUSE/TABLE - DAY

     Martin, Kevin, Jerry, and Chuck are sitting at the table.
     Martin and Jerry are getting into a heated discussion.

                         MARTIN
              All I know I know is that when you
              talk about challenges, you talk about
              basketball.

                         JERRY
              Yeah, if you're talkin' 'bout gettin'
              physical only.

                         MARTIN
              Only? What about strategy? Skill?

                    JERRY
Paintball has all of that. It's like
any other sport.

                    MARTIN
You call paintball a sport? Martin
looks at Jerry in shock.

                    MARTIN (cont'd)
                    (continuing)
You must be crazy!

                    JERRY
It is a sport, man. It gives you
that physical challenge, you have to
work as a team!

                    KEVIN
Give me a break! Paintball. I'd get
more of a physical challenge playing
golf.
Martin and Kevin laugh and high five.

                    CHUCK
                    (low)
Just what I'd expect from him.
A SECRETARY, a shapely White woman,
comes over to talk
to Kevin.

                    SECRETARY
                    (sexily)
Kevin, do you still wanna talk?
Kevin looks her up and down. We SEE
her curvy figure.

                    KEVIN
You know this.
Kevin looks back at the guys.

                    KEVIN (cont'd)
                    (continuing)
Excuse me for a minute, fellas. I
have something I need to take care
of.

Kevin looked at the secretary and then back at the guys.

                    KEVIN (cont'd)
                    (continuing)
Yes, indeed, I think I might have to
take care of this right now.

Kevin gets up and walks away, cockily. Martin pats him on
the back as he leaves.

                    MARTIN
          Oh, she's finally givin' up the
          digits! Kevin's been trying to mack
          her for a long time!

Martin WATCHES Kevin and the secretary walk away MED.
CLOSEUP of Kevin's hand rubbing the secretary's behind.

                    MARTIN (cont'd)
                 (continuing)
          My boy.

We SEE Jerry and Chuck's faces showing mounting distaste.
AL, Martin's friend, enters the break room.

                    MARTIN (cont'd)
          Al!
                 (beat)
          Al!

We SEE Al look in the direction of the voice calling his
name.

                    MARTIN (cont'd)
                 (continuing)
          Over here!

Al smiles and walks over to the table.

                    AL
                 (shaking Martin's
          hand)
          Hey man! What's up?

                    MARTIN
          Sit with us, man! I thought you took
          lunch earlier than this!

Martin looks at his watch.

                    MARTIN (cont'd)
                 (continuing)
          It's damn near three o'clock!

                    AL
          I usually do, but I'm a little late
          today. I've been really busy with
          this being the end of the month. The
          numbers are due and we aren't even
          close to being ready yet. I'm just
          taking a quick break.

                    MARTIN
          You go'n work through lunch?

                     AL
          Yep. And I probably won't get home
          'till late tonight because we have to
          run the reports.

                    MARTIN
          Shit, there ain't no way I'm missin'
          lunch. And if they want me to work
          late, they gotta give me overtime.
          Shit, time and a half, fuck all that.

                     AL
          That's what happens when you're
          salaried.

                    MARTIN
          Yeah, they jerk you.

     Martin looks over at Jerry and Chuck.

                    MARTIN (cont'd)
               (continuing)
          That's okay. I'll take hourly any
          day.

     Jerry and Chuck smirk and mumble in agreement.

                    MARTIN (cont'd)
               (continuing;
                looking at AL)
          They got you right where they want
          you, dawg. You ain't nothin' but a
          slave. When you go'n stop lettin'
          massa beat yo' ass?

     Martin laughs. Jeremy snickers. Chuck's eyes dart

     around the room, trying to ignore the conversation.

                    MARTIN (cont'd)
               (continuing)
          Well, sit with us while you're down
          here. Jerry, Chuck, this is my boy
          Al. He works upstairs in the
          accounting department. This brotha
          here makes sho' we gets paid on time!
               (beat)
          We grew up together.

     Al and Jerry make eye contact.

9.

                    AL
              (shaking their
               hands)
         Good to meet you guys!
              (to Martin)
         ! I have some time to spare. I'll
         sit with you for a couple of minutes.

                  MARTIN
         Cool.

                    AL
         Lemme grab something to drink.

Al goes to get a soda from the soda machine. He LOOKS back
at the table while he puts his dollar in the soda machine.
He SEES Martin talking. Jerry LOOKS up at Al and they make
eye contact. Jerry nods slightly at Al.

Al smirks and looks back at the soda machine. He makes his
selection and GOES back to the table. He sits down next to
Martin.

                  MARTIN
         Kevin'll be back in a few. He's off
         somewhere mackin' that secretary on
         the third floor he's been tryin' ta
         get wit'.

                    AL
         Damn, man. He's constantly checkin'
         the women.

                  MARTIN
         Shit, I ain't mad at him.

Martin sips his soda. Al looks slyly at Jerry and brings
his soda can to his lips.

                    AL
         I know what you mean.

Al sips his soda.

                  CHUCK
         Kevin gets a lot of girls?

                  MARTIN
              (swallowing
               dramatically)
         Does he! Mostly White girls like
         him.

Jerry and Chuck cringe, but Martin doesn't notice.

                    MARTIN (cont'd)
                    (continuing)
                It's 'cause he's a pretty boy.

Chuck LOOKS at Martin.

                    MARTIN (cont'd)
                    (continuing)
                White girls like that, you know.

                    CHUCK
        Really?

                    MARTIN
                    (nudging Al)
                Either that, or they're just tryin'
                to find out if what they say is true!

Martin laughs. Al smiles. Jerry and Chuck patronize him
with a weak chuckle. Martin turns to AL.

                    MARTIN (cont'd)
                    (continuing)
                Did you hear about what happened to
                Jerome and his crew?

                    AL
        No. What happened?

                    MARTIN
                They're dead, man. Cops found 'em
                out in Chantilly, Virginia.

Al shakes his head.

                    MARTIN (cont'd)
                    (continuing)
                Get this shit. Mike was hung. They
                strung him up by his neck, a straight
                up lynching.

                    AL
        What?

                    MARTIN
                Yup. The other guys were shot. The
                cops found them scattered in the
                woods.
                    (beat)
                Somebody took all five of 'em out,
                man!

                              AL
                    Chantilly? What were they doing all
                    the way out there?

                              MARTIN
                    I don't know. Guess we'll never
                    know. The cops think it's drug
                    related, but they think that about
                    everything that happens to Black
                    folks.

                              AL
                    Maybe it was, Martin. Jerome was no
                    saint.

                              MARTIN
                         (staring at Al
                          in disbelief)
                    How could you say that, dawg?

                              AL
                    Because it wouldn't surprise me.
                    People like that are always caught up
                    in it.

                              MARTIN
                    Hold up. What do you mean people
                    like that?

                              AL
                    C'mon, Martin. You know what I'm
                    talking about.

          Al sips his soda.

                              MARTIN
                    No, I don't. How could you lump
                    Jerome in with the hoodrats down in
                    south east?

                              AL
                    Lump him in? He was the ring leader!

                              MARTIN
                    What are you talkin' about? You knew
                    Jerome!

                              AL
                    Yeah, I know. That's what he gets
                    for messing with drugs and trying to
                    live the thug life.

                              MARTIN
                    He never messed with no drugs!

                          AL
               C'mon, man.

                          MARTIN
               He didn't! He was real
               straightforward. Him, Mike, all of
               'em. They were like us.

                          AL
               Oh no. Don't put me in this!

                          MARTIN
               They were just a bunch a guys like us
               who do what they gotta do within the
               law to make ends meet.

We SEE Al LOOK at Martin in disbelief while he speaks. He
reclines in his chair.

                          MARTIN (cont'd)
                        (continuing)
               Even if it means slinging boxes
               around in a hot ass warehouse for a
               livin'. You know what I mean, Jerry?

Martin LOOKS at Jerry. Jerry barely nods.

                          AL
               Within the law?
                        (beat)
               Hmph, if that's what you think.

We SEE the frustration in Martin's face.

                          MARTIN
               What's up wit' you? Why are you so
               down on them?

                          AL
               It's not about them. It's about that
               whole mentality.

                          MARTIN
               I'm tellin' you, Jerome wasn't no
               thug. He was just tryin' to make it.
               Just like me. Unless you sayin' I'm
               a thug!

                          AL
               C'mon Martin, man. You're takin'
               this too far!

                    MARTIN
          I hope so. I bust my ass in this
          warehouse fitty hours a week. But
          it's honest work, and it's betta than
          lookin' over your shoulder for the
          cops or a cap all your life.

                    AL
          Yeah, you say that now!

                    MARTIN
          That's right.
               (beat)
          I admit, I did some shit back in the
          day, but since Tracey got pregnant, I
          been cool.

                    AL
               (low)
          Yeah. A whole seven months.

                    MARTIN
          What?
               (beat)
          What'd you say, man?

                    AL
          I said, then what happened to them,
          Detective Colombo? They walked onto
          a shooting range by mistake?

                    MARTIN
          I don't know, man. But what I do
          know is that whatever happened to
          Jerome and them wasn't about drugs. I
          think it was racism. The Klan,
          maybe.

                    AL
               (laughing)
          The Klan? There you go.

                    MARTIN
          Yeah, man. It's possible.

                    AL
          This is Northern Virginia we're
          talking about. Not Mississippi.

                    JERRY
          Hell, maybe it was. With the hangin'
          and everything.

          Jerry STARES at Al. Al LOOKS back at him, understanding him.

14.

                    MARTIN
            It's not like it couldn't happen out
            here.

Al smirks and looks down at his can, fondling it.

                    AL
            Who knows? You might be right.

Kevin comes back to the table with a smile.

                    KEVIN
            Sorry. I had to get her number right
            quick!
                (seeing Al)
            ! Hey Al! What's goin' on, bruh?

Kevin sits down.

                    KEVIN (cont'd)
                (continuing)
            I ain't seen you in a long time!

                    AL
            Yeah man, I know. I've been really
            busy upstairs.

                    KEVIN
            I guess so! I been busy at the
            office too, if you know what I mean!
                (thumbing the
                 piece of paper)
            ! Maybe I'll call her, maybe I won't.
                (beat)
            You want the digits, Martin? I know
            you don't get much play and I!

                    MARTIN
            I gets mine, okay? Like I need help
            from yo' pretty ass. Women like a
            manly brotha like me.

                    KEVIN
            Yeah, that's why I got the digits and
            you still sittin' here kickin' it
            with the fellas.

Kevin elbows Chuck and laughs. Chuck barely smiles.

                    MARTIN
            Kiss my ass, man.

Jerry has lost his patience.

                    JERRY
          So what about a game, or is it too
          weak for you?

                    AL
          What game?

                    KEVIN
          Are y'all still talkin' that
          paintball shit?

                    MARTIN
               (to Al)
          Jerry wants us to play paintball with
          them. He calls it a sport. Tryin' ta
          play it off like it's some big
          challenge.

                    KEVIN
          What, you want us to play now? It's a
          sucker's game, man. You can't be
          serious.

                    JERRY
          But I am. It's a lot tougher than
          you think it is. Me and the guys go
          up and play just about every weekend.
          We're going up this Saturday to get
          in some rounds. I think it

                    JERRY (cont'd)
          would be a good game. We could even
          put a bet on it ta make thangs
          interesting.

     Jerry pulls out his wallet and shows $100 bill.

                    JERRY (cont'd)
               (continuing)
          Unless money is tight.

     Martin's face becomes tense.

                    KEVIN
          Money is not a problem, believe that.

                    MARTIN
          For a 100 spot? Yeah. Yeah, all
          right, but if we do this I'm addin'
          somethin' to the pot to make it
          sweeter.
                    (MORE)

                    MARTIN (cont'd)
                    (beat)
          If we win, y'all gotta come out and
          sweat it up with the big boys on the
          basketball court.

Jerry and Chuck look at each other. Chuck snickers.

                    MARTIN (cont'd)
                    (continuing)
          Double or nothing on the 100 spot. If
          we lose the paintball game, you get
          the 100 outright. Sound like a deal
          to you?

                    JERRY
          Okay.
                    (beat)
          Okay, fine. If you win, we'll play
          you in basketball, double or nothing
          on the money. If you lose, the money
          is ours.

                    MARTIN
          Sounds like a plan to me. You in
          Kevin?

                    KEVIN
          You know I'm down.

                    MARTIN
          Al?

                    AL
          Saturday? No, I'm not going to be
          able to make it. I have a date.

                    KEVIN
          A date? Nigga please, you know the
          only mack in the crew is yours truly.

                    AL
                    (sighing,
                    getting up)
          Not this time, Kevin. I'll be in
          Baltimore all day with Miss Fine.
          While you all are out playing your
          little kid's game in the woods, I'll
          be otherwise occupied!
                    (walking away)
          ! Take it easy on them. They're
          virgins.

                         MARTIN
            You should be saying that to us! They
            don't want none of me on the court.

                         AL
            Yeah, if it even gets to the court.

                         MARTIN
            All right, boy. We'll see when we
            get back.

We SEE Al walk away. In the F.G. Martin raises his can to
toast the bet. CLOSEUP of the four cans meeting in the
center.

                         JERRY
            You guys don't know what you're in
            for.

                         MARTIN
            Neither do you, Jerry. Neither do
            you.

END FLASHBACK

INT. CHEROKEE - DAY

                         CRAIG
            Whatever, man. We're out here now.
            Craig LOOKS out the window.

We SEE nothing but farmland and desolation.

                         CRAIG (cont'd)
                      (continuing)
            At least we're out somewhere now.

                         MARTIN
            I know this is the right way, unless
            the directions are wrong. Cool out.

INSERT - SIGN ON GROUND

Which reads Pete's Paintball. Next Left.

BACK TO SCENE

Shaun points at the sign and reads it with a southern,
hickish accent.

                         SHAUN
            Pete's Paintball. Next Left. I'm
            guessing that's it.

                    MARTIN
         No shit, Sherlock.
         Martin turns left onto the muddy
         road.
              (continuing)
         Damn! This mud is thick out here!

                    CRAIG
         I'll bet you it's manure.

                    SHAUN
         Yours?

Craig and Shaun playfully tousle in the back seat.

INT. JETTA - DAY

GARY (30), who is clean-cut and polished, is driving the
Jetta. Kevin and ROBERT (28), who wears glasses and is less
vocal, are also in the car. They are all of average build.

Gary sees the mud ahead. He looks at Robert and shakes his
head.

                    GARY
         Tell me he's not going through the
         mud.

                    ROBERT
         Looks like it to me.

                    GARY
         Cherokee - truck. Jetta - car. Am I
         missing something?

                    ROBERT
         You know Martin, man. That car's
         like his dick. He wants to show
         everyone how big it is.
         They laugh.

                    KEVIN
         I say you dust him.

Gary LOOKS at the road and SEES a patch of grass that he can
use to go up the same road.

                    GARY
         Yeah.

We SEE the Jetta pull onto the grass. Gary gives Martin a
look that says, 'you dumb ass'. As he advances up the hill
he BEEPS his horn at the Cherokee.

INT. CHEROKEE - DAY

Martin laughs and follows him on the grass. He rolls down
his window and yells out.

                    MARTIN
          That's what you get for buyin' a toy
          box for a car!

Gary gives Martin the finger in his rear-view mirror.

                    SHAUN
          All I know is that if I'm gonna
          sacrifice my Saturday to spend the
          day finger-painting with y'all
          niggas, I'm for damn sure go'n be the
          best finger-painter out there!

                    CRAIG
          Second only to me, my brotha.
               (beat)
          Too bad Al couldn't make it.

                    SHAUN
          You got to get your play when you
          can. Especially that nigga. Me? I
          gets so much ass, I can afford to
          pass it up here and there. You know?

                    CRAIG
          Shit, if I had a date today, I
          wouldn't be here either.

                    MARTIN
          Yeah! if. Pay attention to that
          word, man. If.

Martin laughs. We SEE Craig and Shaun stare at him.

                    SHAUN
          Listen to this bullshit! Mr. ain't
          seen no parts of the pussy since high
          school! And even then they only gave
          it up to you 'cause you hung wit' me.
          Second best is better than nothin'.
               (beat)
          I guess I just got it like that.

                    MARTIN
          You gotta be kiddin' me!

                         CRAIG
           Shaun, man, you can't live on fantasy
           island all your life. It's not
           healthy.

     Shaun LOOKS at Craig decidedly.

                         SHAUN
           You want some more, don't you?
           Shaun and Craig tousle again.

EXT. RURAL MARYLAND ROAD - DAY

Voice Over of the AD LIB from the Cherokee as Martin, Shaun,
and Craig hype themselves up for the game. Aerial shot of
the Cherokee and the Jetta proceeding up the grass to the
paintball field.

                         MARTIN (V.O.)
           We go'n show Jerry and his boys who's
           runnin' shit up in here. And then we
           go'n take them to the court and spank
           'em for makin' us come all the way
           out here in the first place!

INT. DILAPIDATED HOUSE ON HILL - DAY

The Old Man and The Fourth Man are in the room. The house
is small, sparsely furnished, and old. The Old Man sits in
a recliner full of holes. We SEE The Fourth Man's back, his
face just out of sight. He is standing at the window
looking out through binoculars. He brings the binoculars
from his face and turns to The Old Man, his face still in
the shadows.

                         THE FOURTH MAN
           They're almost here.

                         THE OLD MAN
           Good. Very good. You go down there
           now and get the boys ready. It's
           almost time.

The Fourth Man exits, tossing the binoculars to The Old
Man, still masked in the shadows. The Old Man gets up and
hobbles on his one good leg to the window. He has just
enough time to SEE the tail lights of the Cherokee advance
up the hill.

                         THE OLD MAN (cont'd)
           Here kitty, kitty! C'mon up here and
           get this milk!
                         (MORE)

                    THE OLD MAN (cont'd)
                        (laughing)
                        (roughly)
            !You won't know what hit you. Just a
            little bit closer, now. You almost
            home.

    EXT. PAINTBALL FIELD/ NEUTRAL AREA ONE - DAY

    The Cherokee and Jetta drive as far as they can before
    running into the dense wooded area. Pete is FLAGGING them
    down. Shaun, Martin, Craig, Gary, Kevin, and Robert get out
    of the two cars.

                        PETE
            Hey fellas! Welcome to Pete's
            Paintball field. I'm Pete. You boys
            here to play wit' Jerry?

                        MARTIN
            Yeah.

                        PETE
            Okay then! Park yourselves right
            there and I'll go git the other team
            so we can git started.

                        MARTIN
            Cool, man. Thanks.

    Pete walks back into the woods. Martin tosses the keys

    to the Cherokee to Gary.

                        MARTIN (cont'd)
                        (continuing)
            Here, Gary, before I forget. If I
            lost them in the game, I'd be!

                        GARY
            One pissed muthafucka.

                        MARTIN
            You know it.

    Gary puts the keys into his hip pouch. The guys break off
    and survey the scenery. Robert walks to his left and studies
    the woods.

                        ROBERT
            I don't think I've ever been in woods
            like these.
                        (MORE)

ROBERT (cont'd)
I mean, my grandmother's house has a
little patch of trees in patch of
trees in the back, but the back, but
nothing like this.

GARY
What do you expect? She lives in
North West DC!

They all laugh except Robert. He turns to Gary.

ROBERT
I meant my father's mother. She
lives in Georgia. She's got bonafide
woods behind her house. But not like
this. This is so!

Kevin is standing adjacent to Robert, looking at the woods
also. He is uncharacteristically silent.

KEVIN
Dark.
They all stare at him. He turns back
to the woods.

Craig looks at Martin in the BG. His face questions Kevin's
demeanor. Martin shrugs.

MARTIN
Are we ready to kick some ass?!?

SHAUN
Oh, hell yeah! I can feel the gun in
my hands already.

Shaun holds up an imaginary rifle and fires an imaginary
round. The trees move like they have taken the bullet. He
stares at the trees, bewildered.

MARTIN
All right then! I don't know about
you, but I'm ready to win a game of
B-Ball and 100 bucks for free drinks!
Martin puts his hand out for a team
break.
        (continuing)
Who's down?

Kevin, Robert, Craig, and Gary put their hands on top of
Martin's. Shaun is frozen in place, looking into the trees.
They LOOK over at Shaun.

CRAIG
Hey, man. What's up?

                              SHAUN
                    I don't know, man. I thought -

          Shaun stares closer at the trees and sees nothing.

                              SHAUN (cont'd)
                              (continuing)
                    Nothing. You know I'm wit' it.
                              (beat)
                    Let's do this.

          Shaun puts his hand on top of the others and the team
          breaks. He looks back at the trees over his shoulder. Out
          of nowhere Pete appears at the top of the hill.

                              PETE
                    Hey y'all. Come on up this way. The
                    paintball field is back here a ways.
                    Your friends is waitin' on ya.

          He disappears into the bushes. They start up the hill.

                              KEVIN
                    I guess it's on.

          Martin walks up the hill quickly, passing Kevin while he
          speaks.

                              MARTIN
                    You didn't think they'd wimp out, did
                    you?

                              KEVIN
                              (low)
                    I was kinda hoping they would.

          Shaun catches up to Kevin and HEARS the statement.

                              SHAUN
                    You too?

                              KEVIN
                    When we pulled up I got the strangest
                    feeling. Like someone was watching
                    us, or something.

                              SHAUN
                    I know. I felt something too.
                              (beat)
                    It's just first round jitters, man.
                    That's all it is. We're just
                    trippin'.

```
                     KEVIN
                   (shrugging)
         I know.  But it still spooked me out.
```

Shaun shook his head to shake off the feeling that he shared
with Kevin. He patted Kevin on the back as he advanced up
the hill.

```
                     SHAUN
         C'mon, man.  Let's go.
```

Robert catches up to Martin and looks over his shoulder.

```
                     ROBERT
         I can't even see the car anymore,
         Mart.  We're really going deep in
         here, huh?

                     MARTIN
         Good.  This way we won't hit the cars
         with any paint.
```

Robert shakes his head.

```
                     MARTIN (cont'd)
                   (continuing)
         You know I'd be pissed if I messed up
         my truck.
```

Robert chuckles. They advance up the hill.

EXT. PAINTBALL FIELD/ NEUTRAL AREA TWO - DAY

We SEE Pete and eight other White men standing in the field
waiting. Their names are Jerry, Chuck, KURT, BRAD, EDDIE,
DOUG, WALLY, and STEVE. The White men are all of average
build except Chuck. They are all in their late twenties -
early thirties. The Black men come up the hill and stand in
front of them.

```
                     JERRY
         Martin, glad you and your friends
         made it.  I know it's pretty far out.

                     MARTIN
         We wouldn't have missed this for
         nothin'.

                     JERRY
         You remember Chuck?!
                   (MORE)
```

                         JERRY (cont'd)
                    (pointing at his
                    (guys)
               ! Kurt, Brad, Eddie, Doug, Wally, and
               Steve came along too.

Martin points at his friends.

                         MARTIN
               You know Kevin. This is Shaun, Gary,
               Robert, and Craig. Now that the
               introductions have been made, let's
               get to it.

                         JERRY
               Hold on, now. Looks like we've got
               two more guys than you do. We have
               to even it up to make it a fair game.
               Jerry stretches his hand across his
               team, offering them.
                    (continuing)
               Take your pick.

                         MARTIN
               Okay, cool!
                    (perusing them)
               - All right, how about you?!
                    (pointing)
               - What's your name again, partner?

                         BRAD
                    (snickering,
                    looking at
                    Jerry)
               Brad!
                    (walking towards
                    Martin)
               - Sure, I'm game.

                         JERRY
               All right then! Let's head back so
               we can get this game started.

                         ROBERT
               Back? I thought we were already
               there.

                         JERRY
               Nope. This is just the second
               neutral area. The first neutral
               area's where y'all parked. We gotta
               go further back so we don't disturb
               the folks that live around here!
                    (MORE)

                    JERRY (cont'd)
                  (chuckling,
                  (looking out)
                  - such that there is.

Robert looks uneasy. They go further into the woods to the
ammo station to get guns and ammo. Martin and his friends
are being very cautious.

EXT. PAINTBALL FIELD/ AMMO STATION - DAY

Jerry leans on the wooden, dilapidated counter and throws
his gun onto it. Pete walks behind the counter. Martin
stands next to Jerry.

                       JERRY
              Y'all should probably buy two boxes
              of ammo. You might run out in the
              middle of the game and there's no
              such thing as a break. Load up.

Jerry and his team get their ammo from Pete and walk over to
the common area to load their guns.

                       PETE
              Which ammo can I get y'all?

                       SHAUN
                  (to the guys)
              Which one do you want? The
              fluorescent yellow or those pretty
              little pink balls?

                       KEVIN
              Pink. Now, that's a color I get to
              see a lot of -
                  (walking away)
              - or would that depress y'all too
              much?

Kevin goes to the main paintball field and sits down on a
log, laughing. Gary gives him the finger.

                       GARY
                  (smiling
                  sarcastically)
              Fuck you, you bastard!!
                  (turning to
                  Robert, picking
                  up his gun)
              - Cocky son of a bitch. He's lucky
              he's my boy or else I'd bust a
              fluorescent pink cap in his ass.

Robert laughs. Martin asks for 2 boxes of pink ammo in the
BG while Gary and Robert talk. Martin and Pete exchange
money and Pete gives Martin the ammo.

EXT. PAINTBALL FIELD/ COMMON AREA - DAY

Martin taps Gary and they all sit down and load their guns
while Pete explains the rules of the game.

                    PETE
          Be sho' to keep yo' guns loaded, else
          y'all'll get caught in the fight with
          no ammo. Don't put no ammo that done
          fell on the groun' back in the gun
          'cause it'll jam and you go'n have ta
          come out the game ta fix it. Once
          you come out the game, you cain't go
          back in 'till next round. We plays
          the best of three Capture the Flag.
          You go'n try to take the other team's
          flag off they post and make it back
          to yo' side unharmed. If yo' team do
          dat, you won. If you gets shot once,
          you dead 'till next roun'.

Pete wipes sweat from his brow.

                    PETE (cont'd)
                  (continuing)
          Here is yo' flags !
                  (holding up a
                   red and a yellow
                   bandana)
          - Y'all's forts is opposite each
          other on the field. The field ain't
          nothin' but bushes and trees and
          critters, folks, so watch yo'self out
          there. The game ain't over till the
          flag is captured or there's only one
          man left standing. His team would get
          the roun' if that happen!
                  (throwing the
                   bandanas to the
                   teams)
          - Dis is war, boys. Play to the end.

Pete sits down on the log and lets the teams strategize.

                    SHAUN
          This shit sounds easy! Let's wax
          them real quick and be done with it.

                    ROBERT
          I wonder what's out there, hiding in
          the bushes.

                    CRAIG
          It don't really matter do it? We
          came here to win, and that's exactly
          what we go'n do! Right?

                    KEVIN
          No problem.

                    BRAD
          We need to have one person at the
          fort protecting our flag at all
          times. You know, just in case they
          infiltrate the line somehow.

                    MARTIN
          You know somethin' we don't know,
          Brad? Is that their plan? To drive
          up the middle?
          Brad smiles and shrugs his shoulders.

                    BRAD
          I don't know. As far as I'm
          concerned, they're the enemy this
          time. This is my team.

                    SHAUN
          Don't matter. Ain't nobody coming
          through this here.

                    ROBERT
          I want to be out in the middle of
          things, mixin' it up. I'm tryin' to
          get the flag and bring it home.

          Shaun LOOKS at Robert in disbelief.

                    SHAUN
          You? Hmph, you need to leave the
          game to the big boys. Just sit yo'
          ass down in the bushes and guard the
          fort. Let us handle things.

                    MARTIN
          No, no, Rob really wants to set it
          off!
                    (beat)
          Go for it, man!

          Shaun shakes his head and lifts his hands, giving up.

                    MARTIN (cont'd)
                    (continuing)
          All right, so Rob and Shaun'll go up
          the middle to get the flag. Kevin,
          you and Brad work the sides to
          protect the runners. We need one to
          protect the flag and the rest need to
          cover each other.

                    CRAIG
          I'll hang back and guard the flag.
          Y'all just make sure they don't get
          through. We don't want to have to
          whip out the dogs on 'em.

                    MARTIN
          We'll lock 'em down, don't worry.

                    BRAD
          Sounds good to me.

     We SEE Brad look over at Jerry's team. Martin FOLLOWS his
     stare and SEES the evil look in Jerry's eye.

                    PETE
                    (standing)
          If there ain't no questions, I say
          let's get the game goin'-
                    (looking at Martin's
                    team)
          Y'all boys got any questions?

                    CRAIG
          No, we're straight.

                    PETE
          All right then. When I blow dis
          whistle once you got two minutes to
          find yo' hidin' spot. When I blow it
          again, the game will start. All
          right?
                    (beat)
          Ready?
                    (beat)
          One!
                    (beat)
          Two!
                    (beat)
          Three!

     Pete blows the whistle. Martin is STARING at Jerry who
     STARES back. Martin is getting mad.

                    KEVIN
          Martin -
                    (walking over to
                    him)
          - Martin! What's up? We gotta get
          our spots before he blows the whistle
          again.
                    MARTIN
          It's Jerry!

Kevin LOOKS at Jerry. Jerry smiles and salutes them.

                    KEVIN
          What about him?

                    MARTIN
          I'm tellin' you. He was starin' me
          down. Like he wanted to start
          somethin'.

                    KEVIN
          You're seein' things.

                    MARTIN
          Maybe!

                    KEVIN
          Let's go, before we get shot.

                    MARTIN
          Yeah, let's get this party started
          right.

EXT. PAINTBALL FIELD/ MAIN - DAY

They find their hiding places and crouch down into the
bushes.

The second whistle BLOWS.

                    KEVIN
                    (whispering to
                    Gary)
          I can't see any of them. You?

                    GARY
          No. I'm gonna move closer to get a
          better look.

                    KEVIN
                    (smiling)
          Go 'head, Rambo!

Gary advances. We SEE Robert advance toward the other team.
Kurt makes himself visible b.g. across the field.

Kevin takes aim on Kurt. Brad aims at Kevin's head through
the trees f.g..

                        KEVIN (cont'd)
            Just let me get a clean shot off!
                    (loosening his
                    crouch)
            - Yeah, I see you!
                    (aiming)
            - I got you, baby, don't you worry.

Kevin shoots a couple of rounds of paint and misses as Kurt
disappears into the bushes. Kevin sinks back into his
hiding spot. Brad leans in.

                        BRAD
            No, I got you.

O.S. the CRACK of the shotgun. We SEE Shaun and Robert duck
at the sound.

                        SHAUN
            Did you hear that? It sounded like
            gunfire. Real gunfire, man!

                        ROBERT
                    (standing)
            What the fuck is going on, man?

A SHOT pierces Robert's throat. SLOW MOTION as we SEE the
blood spray on Shaun. AD LIB Jerry's team hooting and
hollering in glee. High fives SLAPPING.

                        MARTIN
                    (low)
            Oh shit! Oh, holy shit!

Craig looks through the bushes and SEES Brad blowing the
barrel of his rifle like it was smoking. Wally pats him on
the back.

                        CRAIG
            That son of a bitch led them right to
            us!

                        JERRY
            Now, that's what I call a game!

Loud LAUGHTER and boisterous activity.

                         JERRY (cont'd)
                        (continuing)
            I hope y'all like it, 'cause it's
            suitin' me just fine. Try and enjoy
            it, if you can. It'll be the last
            game you ever play, after all.

                         SHAUN
            You bastard! When I catch you!

                         JERRY
            When you catch me?
                        (beat)
            You dumb muthafucka, you won't catch
            me. The question is,
                        (beat)
            when will I catch you?
                        (beat)
            Rest up now. You never know when
            I'll be comin' for ya.

Jerry turns and starts to walk away. He stops an turns
back.

                         JERRY (cont'd)
                        (continuing)
            Oh, Martin! About that 100 dollars?
            Keep it. I'd do this for free any
            day.

Jerry and his team are LAUGHING. Martin erupts into a
painfully guttural SCREAM, his head upturned to the sky.

EXT. PAINTBALL FIELD/ MAIN - DAY

Martin, Shaun, Craig, and Gary are sitting together, hidden
within the bushes.

                         CRAIG
            I think they're gone.

                         SHAUN
            They're still out there, waiting to
            take us out.

                         GARY
            What the fuck is going on, man?

Martin SEES the blood on Shaun's shirt.

                         MARTIN
            Are you hurt, Shaun?

                          SHAUN
              It's - it's Rob's.

                          GARY
              This shit can't be happening!

                          SHAUN
              I saw him! I saw Robert go down, man.

Martin sinks his head.

                          SHAUN (cont'd)
                          (continuing)
              I couldn't help him!

                          GARY
              I had just walked away from Kevin to
              get a better look. It couldn't have
              been more than a minute!

We SEE Shaun touch the blood on his sweatshirt. He lifts
his hand to his face and SEES the blood.

                          GARY (cont'd)
                          (continuing;
                          low)
              It wasn't more than a minute.

INT. DILAPIDATED HOUSE ON HILL - DAY

Jerry has come to the house and is talking to The Old Man
and The Fourth Man, who is facing the window.

                          THE OLD MAN
              Where are they now?

                          JERRY
              In the field. Scared shitless. They
              don't have a chance in hell.

We SEE The Fourth Man's face as he turns to Jerry. The
Fourth Man will heretofore be called Al.

                          AL
              They do if you stay up here talking
              to us.

                          JERRY
              Who the fuck are you to tell me what
              to do, boy?

Jerry bucks up against Al, but The Old Man intervenes.

```
                    THE OLD MAN
              He's right, Jerry. Don't stay up
              here too long. They could figure out
              how to get out of the woods.

                    JERRY
              There's no way they can get out. By
              now they're so twisted around, they
              wouldn't know which way was up if we
              pointed to it. It's cool.

                    AL
              Don't underestimate them, Billy Bob.
              They're not like the other ones.
              These guys aren't stupid. You need to
              take them out quickly. If you don't -
                    (looking out the
                    window; beat)
              - then I will.
```

EXT. PAINTBALL FIELD/ MAIN - DAY

Martin, Shaun, Craig, and Gary are sitting and planning.

```
                    CRAIG
              We have to get out of here. They're
              gonna wipe us out, and quickly, if we
              don't come up with a plan.

                    SHAUN
              He's right. We're easy pickin's just
              sittin' here. We have to get moving.

                    MARTIN
              Okay. Our guns are garbage. They
              have real guns, that much we know.

                    SHAUN
              Yeah, our guns ain't worth shit.
```

Shaun throws his gun at a tree. It SMASHES.

```
                    GARY
              They all cleared out with Jerry. I
              watched each and every one of them
              leave through the bushes. If I had a
              gun, I'd have!

                    SHAUN
              I know, man. Me too.
```

                    CRAIG
          Look, we can't deal in woulda and
          coulda right now. We have to figure
          out how to get the hell out of here.

                    MARTIN
          We have to split up.

                    GARY
          What?

                    SHAUN
          He's right. If we move in a pack
          it'll be easier for them to take us
          out all at once.

                    MARTIN
          We have to make our way to the
          neutral area quietly and quickly.

                    CRAIG
          Right. When we get to the cars, we
          get in, sit on the floor, and wait
          for the rest of the group.

Gary shakes his head and sighs.

                    CRAIG (cont'd)
                 (continuing)
          When everybody's in, we'll put the
          car in neutral and roll down that
          hill we came up. We won't turn the
          car on until we get close to the
          road.

                    SHAUN
                 (nodding)
          So they'll have to run to catch us.

                    CRAIG
          Right.

                    GARY
          That will never work! They probably
          have the cars covered right now.
          They know that would be the first
          thing we'd think to do. They're just
          waitin' for us to make a fool move
          like that so they can cut us down.

                    MARTIN
          You got a better plan?

                    SHAUN
        We have to run for it, Gary. There's
        no other choice! What are we gonna
        do? Just sit here and let them blow
        us away? It's free target practice!

                    GARY
        Like running isn't? Why don't we
        just hand them our asses, and call it
        a day, while we're at it?

                    CRAIG
        C'mon man!

Shaun is angry. He gets in Gary's face.

                    SHAUN
        Why don't I hand them your ass as a
        peace offering? Maybe that'll get
        the rest of us outta here.

                    GARY
        I'd like to see you try, muthafucka.

                    MARTIN
        Enough of this bullshit! Now ain't
        the time for you two to piss on each
        other. We have to get the fuck outta
        here. You wanna die in this trap?

                    SHAUN
        Naw, baby. I ain't goin' out like
        that. I'm not gonna die out here.

                    CRAIG
        Nobody else is gonna die here, man.
        We just have to stick to the plan,
        all right? If they have the cars
        covered, we'll go to plan B.

                    GARY
        What's plan B?

                    CRAIG
        Run for the road.

                    GARY
        Are you crazy? You know they got
        that covered!

                    CRAIG
        They got everything covered, man.
                    (MORE)

CRAIG (cont'd)
(beat)
They're serious about this shit. This
ain't no game. It's war, and We're
runnin' through here unarmed. All we
can do is run.

GARY
We're runnin' right into their trap,
man.

SHAUN
What the hell you think this is?

CRAIG
Not if we use the outskirts. They
can't be that deep in the bushes.
It's a gamble, but we don't have any
other choice if we want to get out of
here.

SHAUN
And I'm for damned sure getting out
of here.

CRAIG
We all are.

MARTIN
Look, if there's any trouble, whistle
three times. We all have to keep our
ears open for that whistle. We
should meet back here if something
happens so we can regroup.

GARY
Yeah. All except the one who
whistled.

CRAIG
Look man, we're all scared. But we
gotta concentrate on getting out of
here instead of talkin' like we
won't. Okay?

SHAUN
Let him stay his punk ass here if he
wants. Killing him'll slow them down
and give us more time to get out.

CRAIG
Shaun!

                         SHAUN
              Naw, man. I'm tired of wastin' time
              on this fool. Let him do what he
              wants.
                         GARY
              All right, all right! I'll go.
              Anything'll be better than sittin'
              here, waitin' to die.
                         SHAUN
              Don't do us no favors.
                         CRAIG
              Lay off, man.

Shaun shakes his head in disgust.

                         MARTIN
                    (listening)
              All right, we better split up now.
              It's getting too quiet out here.
                         CRAIG
              Okay, remember the plan and we'll be
              home free.
                    (beat)
              Good luck to us.

We SEE them break up and scatter.

INT. DILAPIDATED HOUSE ON HILL - DAY

Al looks through his binoculars at the group breaking up and
moving in different directions.

                         AL
              Let the games begin.

EXT. PAINTBALL FIELD/ THICK ONE - DAY

Martin is making his way through the bushes quietly. He sees
a wounded person up ahead sitting on the ground with his
back facing him. The wounded person is Al.

Martin starts to run in the other direction. Al breathing
heavily.

                    AL
          Kevin? Martin? That you? Oh God!
               (curling into a
               ball)
          - help me!
               (barely audible;
               beat)
          - Help me, please.

Martin looks for protection as he goes to the wounded man.
He picks up a rock and crawls behind him.

                    MARTIN
          I will blow your head off,
          muthafucka, so don't fuck wit' me.
          Who are you?

                    AL
          Martin?
               (reaching
               towards Martin)
          Is that you, man?

                    MARTIN
          Al? What the hell?!
               (approaching Al)
          ! What happened to you, man?

                    AL
          I was calling out to you.
               (beat)
          I just wanted to play.

                    MARTIN
               (crouching, holding
               Al)
          Where are you hurt?

                    AL
          They came at me from out of nowhere.
          I -
               (doubling over)
          - I didn't see the gun.

                    MARTIN
          Okay. Okay. Let me see it, man.
          Everything's gonna be all right. Let
          me put pressure on the shot.

                    AL
               (rocking)
          They came at me so fast, I -

Martin tries to put his hand over the wound. Al will not let
him see it. There isn't any blood on Al but he looks like
he is suffering.

                    MARTIN
          It's a war zone out here, man.

                    MARTIN
          They're trying to kill us! All we
          have is those fuckin' paint balls to
          shoot and they're shootin' caps at
          us! Robert and Kevin -
               (beat)
          - They're dead, man.
               (beat)
          They're dead.

                    AL
          No! Dear God, no! This can't be
          happening.

                    MARTIN
          I know, man. We gotta get outta here
          or we're all gonna be dead soon.
          C'mon man, try to get up.

Martin helps Al to his feet while he speaks.

                    MARTIN (cont'd)
               (continuing)
          You shoulda stayed in Baltimore with
          your girl. How'd you know where we
          were, anyway? Hell, we in the middle
          of nowhere!

Al starts LAUGHING demonically. He pulls a GUN from his
jacket and points it at Martin.

                    AL
          I was wondering when you'd get around
          to that.

                    MARTIN
          What the fuck?

                    AL
          You dumb muthafucka! I'll bet you
          thought this was gonna be an easy
          win, didn't you? Y'all couldn't wait
          to get that $100 so you could spend
          it on malt liquor or some other
          garbage.

Martin is shocked and upset.

AL (cont'd)
          (continuing)
Not this time. See, I'm runnin' this
shit, and I say it's time that niggas
like you lose.

                    MARTIN
You son of a bitch! You in on this
shit!

                    AL
He's a genius, ladies and gentlemen!
Didn't take you nearly as long as
Jerome and his crew.

                    MARTIN
What? You took Jerome and them out?

                    AL
Bingo! You aren't as stupid as I
thought!

                    MARTIN
What kinda shit are you on, bruh?

                    AL
Reality, baby. One dose'll open your
eyes wide so you can see the world
for what it really is. Too much of
it'll kill ya.

                    MARTIN
What the hell are you talkin' about,
man?

                    AL
What am I talkin' about? I'm talkin'
about me livin' and you dyin', my
brotha.

                    MARTIN
We're supposed to be boys.

                    AL
Boys? I'm a man, Martin. A man. Do
you have any idea what that means? I
work for a living. Real work.
Meaningful work. Not some lowly
stock boy junk that you all think is
such big shit. I use my mind, not my
body to get the job done.

                         MARTIN
            So that makes you better than us,
            right?

                         AL
            You tell me? Can you do what I do?
            Can you walk in my shoes? All y'all
            ever think about is how much pussy
            you can get and what you're gonna do
            on Friday night. That's not what
            real life is made of.
                    (beat)
            You couldn't last a day being me.

                         MARTIN
            Why would I want to? I'm fine like I
            am.

                         AL
            Yeah, if being a shiftless nigger is
            fine by you.

                         MARTIN
            Nigga, I work for a living too.

     Al SHAKES his head.

                         MARTIN (cont'd)
                    (continuing)
            No, it may not be behind a desk in
            some office building, but I do work.

                         AL
            Yeah, because of me. You wouldn't
            even be working at the warehouse if I
            didn't get you the job.

                         MARTIN
            So you're sayin' I can't make my own
            way?

                         AL
            Now you're catching on.

                         MARTIN
            I can't believe this shit!

                         AL
            Believe it.

                         MARTIN
            I remember when you didn't have that
            job. I remember when you didn't have
            that degree and those clothes.
                    (MORE)

                    MARTIN (cont'd)
          I remember when you was crew. You
          get up wit' them White Boys in
          corporate America and you think you
          one of them! So, now you go'n take
          us out 'cause we not exactly like
          you? We ain't good enough?
                    (beat)
          We ain't White enough? What makes
          you think that what you are is right?

                    AL
          Funny, I could ask you the same
          question.

                    MARTIN
          What?

                    AL
          Isn't that what you do to me? Don't
          you think that, somehow, you are
          better than me? I'm a slave and I
          think I'm one of those White boys, do
          you remember when you said that? The
          countless times you've said that? Or
          how about when you said that I was
          soft and I couldn't play basketball
          because I wasn't really Black. Do
          you remember all that shit, Martin?

          Martin sighs and mumbles.

                    AL (cont'd)
                    (continuing)
          No, do you? Since we were kids I've
          had to put up with you demeaning me.
          You were trying to oppress me, to

                    AL
          control me, the same way you say the
          White man tries to control you. I
          think it's because I've always been
          smarter than you all.

                    MARTIN
          That's what you think, huh?

                    AL
          I do. What other reason could you
          have? You knew I would be on top in
          life and you wanted to try to bring
          me down before I got there or ride my
          coat tails on the way up. Only I was
          too naive to see it back then.
                    (MORE)

44.

                    AL (cont'd)
            When I think of all the shit y'all
            put me through it makes me sick.

                    MARTIN
            You ain't the only one gettin' sick
            up in here.

                    AL
            See? Always a funny man. Even now.

                    MARTIN
            What the hell are you talkin' about,
            man? We were kids!

                    AL
            Is that your excuse? Constantly you
            downed me, ridiculed me, and tried to
            make me think that I wasn't as cool
            or as popular or as down as you were.
            That shit's not important to me now.

                    MARTIN
            Isn't it, though? If it wasn't, you
            wouldn't be doin' this shit. Who you
            think you go'n impress on Death Row?

                    AL
            You got it all wrong. I'm not doing
            this to impress anyone, and I won't
            serve time for it, either. That's
            what this White trash is out here
            for. I'm doing this for me. I'm
            doing what has to be done for my
            people.

                    MARTIN
            Your people? So I ain't Black now?
            Or are you claimin' oreos now?

                    AL
            That's just like you. I'm talking
            about real Black people. Your skin
            is black, yeah. I know you think
            you're Black, in some ghetto way. But
            a real Black man wouldn't let the
            doors that were opened for us by
            people like King and Evers and X slam
            shut in his face.

        Martin shakes his head in disbelief.

                    MARTIN
            I can't believe this shit, man.

                              AL
                        (talking louder)
                  A real Black man wouldn't let
                  opposition stop him, and blame the
                  missed opportunity on the White man.
                  You think livin' in the streets and
                  just making ends meet is the way life
                  is, the way it's supposed to be. I
                  say that's barely livin' at all.

Al paces.

                              AL (cont'd)
                        (continuing)
                  You'd rather be given everything you
                  get rather than work for it yourself.
                  Niggers like you bring hard-working,
                  strong-minded Black people down. So,
                  no, you're not Black. You're nothing
                  but a nigger.

                              MARTIN
                  Is that somethin' you learned from
                  those White boys you hang out with?

                              AL
                  Nigga please!

                              MARTIN
                  I'm only go'n be but so many of yo'
                  niggas.

                              AL
                  But you are a nigger. You're
                  ignorant. That's what the word
                  means, in case you didn't know.
                  You're a nigger, and so are these
                  hicks out here playing paintball with
                  you.

                              MARTIN
                  And you the biggest nigga out of all
                  of us.

Martin acts like he's going to attack Al. Al cocks the gun.

                              AL
                  You betta cool out , man, 'cause I
                  will shoot your ass.

Martin WHISTLES three times, staring at Al.

                          AL (cont'd)
                        (continuing)
                What the hell is that? Some kind of
                code?

                          MARTIN
                Maybe.
                        (beat)
                Maybe not.
                        (beat)
                Big man wit' a gun.
                        (beat)
                You betta do somethin' with it or
                I'll take it from you and shoot yo'
                ass, bitch.

                          AL
                Gotta play hard till the end, huh?

                          MARTIN
                I ain't playin'.

Al LOOKS into Martin's eyes and we SEE Al pull the trigger.
Martin is dead.

                          AL
                Neither am I.

EXT. PAINTBALL FIELD/ THICK TWO - DAY

Craig stops short when he hears the WHISTLE, panting. The
SHOT rings out.

                          CRAIG
                Oh my God.

Craig turns back and runs toward the main paintball field.

EXT. PAINTBALL FIELD/ THICK THREE -DAY

Shaun stops short when he hears the WHISTLE and looks
around. He turns to run back to the main paintball field.
The SHOT rings out.

                          SHAUN
                Oh shit.

EXT. PAINTBALL FIELD/ NEUTRAL AREA ONE - DAY

Gary stops short when he hears the WHISTLE then SHOOTS. He
covers his ears and sinks to his knees.

Panting, he looks through the branches and SEES the cars.
Gary looks over his shoulder and then back at the CARS. He
PUTS his hand in his hip pouch and pulls OUT the keys. He
clinches the keys in his hand and LOOKS at the cars again.

                         GARY
              Fuck this.

Gary looks back one more time, guilty.

                         GARY (cont'd)
                      (continuing)
              I'm goin'.

Gary runs out of the woods to the cars.

EXT. PAINTBALL FIELD/ THICK ONE - DAY

Al turns around to walk away and Eddie is standing behind
him. Eddie STARES at Al hard. Al is nervous because he
thinks Eddie overheard him talking to Martin.

                         AL
              Hey man. I just got one.

Eddie stares through him.

                         EDDIE
              So I see.

Eddie walks away, still staring at Al. When Eddie is out of
sight Al shakes his head.

EXT. PAINTBALL FIELD/ MAIN - DAY

Shaun and Craig arrive at the main paintball field at the
same time, panting and out of breath.

                         SHAUN
              Did you hear that gunshot?

                         CRAIG
              Yeah, I did.
                      (beat)
              I heard someone whistle, too.

                         SHAUN
                      (sitting down)
              So did I -
                      (wiping sweat
                      from his brow)
              - Who do you think it was?

                              CRAIG
                        I don't know, man.

         Craig looks out into the woods.

                              CRAIG (cont'd)
                              (continuing)
                        I just wish Gary and Martin would
                        hurry the fuck up.

         EXT. DILAPIDATED HOUSE ON THE HILL - DAY

         The house is old and run down. The shingles are loose, some
         are gone. It is a condemned, lackluster rambler.

         EXT. DILAPIDATED HOUSE ON THE HILL - DAY

         We SEE Al approach the door. O.S. mumbling, talking. He
         puts his ear to the door.

                              EDDIE (O.S.)
                        I heard him sayin' somethin' like
                        that. I told you that nigger was
                        trouble.

                              THE OLD MAN (O.S.)
                        We'll handle him, don't you worry.

         INT. DILAPIDATED HOUSE ON THE HILL - DAY

         AD LIB mumbling as Al enters the room. The Old Man and
         Eddie stop talking. Eddie pats The Old Man on the shoulder
         and exits the house. Before he leaves he snickers at Al.

                              AL
                        What was that all about?

                              THE OLD MAN
                        The boys is gettin' restless. They
                        want to turn up the heat a bit...
                              (shifting)
                        ... I tol' them to go ahead, but keep
                        it quiet.

         The Old Man hobbles to the window.

                              THE OLD MAN (cont'd)
                              (continuing)
                        Ain't seen Joe yet so I don't know
                        what kind a buffer we got.

>   AL
>   You don't think Joe skipped out on
>   us, do you?

>   THE OLD MAN
>   Hell no! I'm just playin' it safe,
>   is all.

Al looks back at the door, pondering what he heard.

>   THE OLD MAN (cont'd)
>   (continuing)
>   Where you been? You took off like a
>   bat outta hell.

>   AL
>   I went out to get one of them.

>   THE OLD MAN
>   You? Didn't figure you for pullin'
>   the trigger.

>   AL
>   Don't ever underestimate me.

>   THE OLD MAN
>   You tough shit, huh?
>   (beat)
>   Guess them boys didn't mean nothin'
>   to ya?

>   AL
>   (beat)
>   They were my friends.

>   THE OLD MAN
>   Shit! I'd hate to see what you do to
>   yo' enemies!

The Old Man starts LAUGHING as Al exits silently. The Old
Man WATCHES him leave.

>   THE OLD MAN (cont'd)
>   Don't underestimate me either, boy.

EXT. PAINTBALL FIELD/ NEUTRAL AREA ONE - DAY

Gary makes his way down to the cars, crouching.

>   GARY
>   You can make it! You can make it!

When he makes it to the Jetta he hides. He sprints to the
Cherokee. Kneeling, he takes the keys OUT of his pocket.
He fumbles with them, trying to find the right one to fit
the lock.

                    GARY (cont'd)
                    (continuing)
          C'mon, c'mon, c'mon -

He FINDS the right key.

                    GARY (cont'd)
                    (continuing)
          Yes!

He puts the key in the lock and UNLOCKS it. Before he opens
the door he HEARS the cock of a gun behind him. He freezes
in terror, his hand still on the keys in the lock.

                    EDDIE
          Looks like I caught me a nigger.

                    GARY
                    (stuttering)
          You - you don't have to do this, man.
          You don't have to kill me.

                    EDDIE
          What? What'd you say, boy? Turn
          'round and face me sos I can hear yo'
          last words clearly.

Eddie pushes the barrel of the gun into Gary's head, using
it to turn him around. Gary TAKES the keys out of the door.
Gary faces Eddie nervously.

                    EDDIE (cont'd)
          Now, what'd you say boy?

                    GARY
          I said you don't have to kill me. We
          can work something out!

                    EDDIE
          Work somethin' out? Like what?

                    GARY
          I got money.

Eddie laughs.

                    GARY (cont'd)
          I do. Look!

Gary digs into his pockets to find money for Eddie. He
comes up with only his license, some gum, a condom, a bank
card, and $20. Eddie LAUGHS loudly.

                         EDDIE
               Twenty dollars? That all yo' life's
               worth to ya? Or is you holdin' out
               on ole Eddie?

Eddie moves closer into Gary's face.

                         GARY
               No, man!

                         EDDIE
               See, I know you got money, boy. You
               and yo' friends got a lot of money.
               Sellin' crack got to get you mo' than
               twenty dollars.

                         GARY
               Sellin' crack? I don't sell drugs.

                         EDDIE
               Yeah, right. And I'm a Puerto Rican
               spic.

                         GARY
               Think what you want, but I don't. Is
               that what this is about?

                         EDDIE
               Nope. This is 'bout you bein' a
               dirty nigger.

                         GARY
               C'mon man. We can work this out. I
               got more money than this. It's just
               not on me.

                         EDDIE
               And what do Eddie got to do wit'
               that?

                         GARY
                    (beat)
               Take me into town, to a bank. I can
               get you more money. How much do you
               want? You can take it all.

                         EDDIE
               You think I'm stupid, boy? You think
               I'm go'n take you to town so's you
               can get the police on me?

                                GARY
                It wouldn't be like that, man. We
                could just forget all this happened.

                                EDDIE
                Oh yeah?

                                GARY
                Yeah!

        Eddie stops laughing and his face became cold.

                                EDDIE
                There ain't no amount of money you
                could give me to stop me from killin'
                you, nigger.

        Gary's eyes plead with Eddie. Eddie aims his gun.

                                GARY
                No, man. Don't do it.

                                EDDIE
                I'm sendin' you straight to hell,
                where you belong, nigger.

        Gary shields his face with his arms.

                                GARY
                Nooooo!

        Eddie SHOOTS Gary in the head. Gary falls against the c and
        onto the ground with an unnerving THUMP. We SEE Eddie reach
        down and pluck the keys from Gary's dead hand. Chuckling,
        he walks away.

        EXT. PAINTBALL FIELD/ MAIN - DAY

        Craig and Shaun hear the SHOT. They look up and around.

                                SHAUN
                Oh shit.
                        (beat)
                Who do you think that was?

                                CRAIG
                I don't know man. What I do know is
                that we gotta get the fuck outta here
                before they take us all out.

        Craig and Shaun get up.

                    SHAUN
          Shouldn't we wait for the others!

                    CRAIG
          We can't wait! Someone else just got
          shot, man! If we wait around we're
          just gonna get shot too.

                    SHAUN
          Your right, man. We gotta go.

                    CRAIG
          The plan's still the same. Make a
          run for the cars and get in. This
          time drive that muthafucka outta
          here. Don't wait.

                    SHAUN
          What? I'm not leaving you here if I
          get to the cars first! I'm go'n wait
          on the floor like we said.

                    CRAIG
          No, Shaun. It's way too risky now.
          These guys are serious. They're
          pickin' us off one by one. We have
          to get outta here if we get the
          chance.

                    SHAUN
          But what about you?

                    CRAIG
          Who say's you'll get to the cars
          before me? Besides, I still know how
          to hot wire a car. I'll take the
          Jetta if the Cherokee is gone.

Shaun hangs his head.

                    CRAIG (cont'd)
                    (continuing)
          We're both gonna get outta here, man.
          I'll see you later on tonight and
          we'll chill over a beer.

                    SHAUN
          I think I'm go'n need somethin' a
          little stronger than that!

Craig and Shaun laugh. Shaun gets serious.

                        SHAUN (cont'd)
                        (continuing)
                 All right man. Let's do this.

Shaun and Craig shake hands.

                        CRAIG
                 Be careful man.

Craig points at Shaun.

                        CRAIG (cont'd)
                        (continuing)
                 Hey, don't be a hero. Just get your
                 ass to the car and get the fuck outta
                 here.

                        SHAUN
                 You askin' too much man.

                        CRAIG
                 Later, man. We'll get their asses
                 after we get out of this trap.
                 Believe me. They'll pay for this
                 shit.

                        SHAUN
                 You ain't sayin' nothin' but a word.

They release each other's hands. They move in opposite
directions. Shaun turns around.

                        SHAUN (cont'd)
                        (continuing)
                 Don't be late tonight. Ten o'clock
                 at the crib.

                        CRAIG
                 I'll bring the pizza.

They run off.

INT. DILAPIDATED HOUSE ON THE HILL - DAY

The Old Man is sitting in a chair facing the window. Jerry
is in the room with Chuck and Eddie.

                        THE OLD MAN
                 How many more of 'em are out there?

                        EDDIE
                 Just two of 'em now. I took one of
                 'em out by the cars.

Eddie holds up the keys and jingles them.

                    EDDIE (cont'd)
                    (continuing)
          They won't be goin' nowhere now.

                    THE OLD MAN
          Good. I want you to take that yellow
          nigger out too.

                    CHUCK
          Al?

                    THE OLD MAN
          Yeah. He's gettin' to big for his
          britches. He thinks he's runnin'
          this here game, and I'm 'bout tired
          of it.

                    JERRY
          Leave that nigger to me. I been
          waitin' a long time to take him out.
                    (beat)
          He's mine.

                    THE OLD MAN
          Make sure you kill him in front of
          those other niggers. Let 'em see who
          he really is before they all die.

                    CHUCK
          Fuckin' sell out bastard. We should
          let him loose out there and let them
          deal wit' 'im. You know they'll kill
          'im for sure.

                    JERRY
          No, no. This boy is mine. Go on and
          git 'im for me, boys. I'll be here
          waitin' for him. Don't beat him up
          too bad. I want him awake for this
          shit.

EXT. PAINTBALL FIELD/ THICK THREE - DAY

Shaun moves quietly within the woods. He HEARS voices ahead
of him. O.S. chatter. He stops running and hides.

Kurt and Brad are standing in the woods talking. They have
their guns at their sides. Kurt is smoking a cigarette.

                    BRAD
          Have you bagged one yet?

                          KURT
          Nope. They're running like racin'
          dogs. E'ry time I think I got one,
          he take off.

                          BRAD
          Niggas is good for runnin', you know.

Kurt nods his head yes.

                          BRAD (cont'd)
                          (continuing)
          Dis yo' first time on a hunt?

                          KURT
          Yup.

                          BRAD
          Give it time, then. You'll git one
          sooner than later.

                          KURT
          Yeah. Don't you worry. I'm go'n git
          one of 'em today. Cain't let you be
          the only one to have fun.

                          BRAD
          Yeah, I got mine early. But I been
          doin' this for a while now. This is
          my fifteenth hunt. Hell, I been in
          'bout thirty-two rounds.

                          KURT
          You an old head then!

                          BRAD
          Yeah, but not too old to catch me a
          nigger or two.

They laugh.

                          BRAD (cont'd)
                          (continuing)
          I think I'm go'n head back to the
          house and wait 'till the second
          round.

Shaun's face grimacces in disgust. He shifts in the bushes.
Kurt and Brad HEAR the movement. They whisper.

                          BRAD (cont'd)
                        (continuing;
                         pointing)
                    Hell, you might got you one right
                    there!

                          KURT
                    I just might.

                          BRAD
                    Well go'n an' git it. I'll see you
                    back at the house.

                          KURT
                    Okay.

SERIES OF SHOTS

A) WE FOLLOW KURT AS HE APPROACHES THE BUSHES.

B) SHAUN LAYS ON HIS STOMACH AND WATCHES KURT COME.

C) SHAUN THROWS A ROCK TO HIS LEFT AND IT LANDS WITH A
THUMP.

D) KURT ADVANCES TO THE BUSHES ON HIS RIGHT CAUTIOUSLY.

E) SHAUN LEAPS OUT OF THE BUSHES AND ONTO KURT, SLAMMING HIM
INTO A TREE. THE CIGARETTE FALLS FROM HIS MOUTH AND HE
DROPS HIS GUN.

F) SHAUN PUNCHES KURT IN THE JAW.

G) KURT KICKS SHAUN IN THE BALLS AND SHAUN DOUBLES OVER.

H) IN THE B.G. THE CIGARETTE HAS STARTED A FIRE. IT IS
SMALL.

I) SHAUN THROWS DIRT INTO KURT'S EYES.

J) KURT STUMBLES AND FALLS BACKWARDS INTO THE FIRE.

K) KURT SCREAMS AND ROLLS, EXTINGUISHING THE FIRE. WHEN HE
OPENS HIS EYES, SHAUN IS STANDING OVER HIM WITH HIS GUN.

                          SHAUN
                    Look what I caught. A flame-broiled
                    White boy.

                          KURT
                    Take that gun off me, nigger.

                          SHAUN
                    No please? Where are your manners?

                    KURT
          I said!

                    SHAUN
          I know what you said. And I don't
          care. I want you to tell me what
          this is all about.

                    KURT
          Fuck you, nigger.

Shaun cocks the gun.

                    SHAUN
          What did you say?

                    KURT
          You don't scare me, boy. I've dealt
          with a lot worse than you.

                    SHAUN
          Doesn't look like you'll be dealing
          with anyone else ever again, though,
          does it? Now tell me what this is
          all about and maybe I'll let your
          family live.

                    KURT
                (beat)
          You don't know nothin' 'bout my
          family!

                    SHAUN
          Not yet, but I've got the gun. Give
          me your wallet.

                    KURT
          What?

                    SHAUN
          Give me your wallet!

                    KURT
          You go'n have ta shoot me, monkey.

Shaun shoots Kurt in the leg. Kurt grabs it and YELLS.

                    SHAUN
          Now, give me your wallet. I'm not
          go'n ask you again.

Kurt gives his wallet to Shaun. Shaun takes out his license
and a picture of a woman and a child.

59.

INSERT - BACK OF PICTURE WHICH READS SARA AND LESLIE JANE.

BACK TO SCENE

                    SHAUN (cont'd)
                    (continuing)
          Sara and Leslie Jane. Looks like I
          know all I need to know about your
          family now, Mr. Kurt Reilly of 1801
          Decatur Street.

                    KURT
          Oh God.
                    (beat)
          What do you want to know?

                    SHAUN
          I thought that'd get your attention.

Kurt LOOKS disgusted.

                    SHAUN (cont'd)
                    (continuing)
          What the fuck is goin' on here? What
          kind of game are y'all playin' and
          why am I caught up in it?

                    KURT
          It's not a game, boy. It's justice.

                    SHAUN
          Don't fuck wit' me, man. Or Sara and
          Leslie Jane'll pay.

Shaun takes aim.

                    KURT
                    (frantically)
          We brought y'all out here to kill
          you. It's what we do.

                    SHAUN
          What do you mean, it's what you do?

                    KURT
          We call this field here the black
          hole 'cause niggers come down here
          and never come back out.

                    SHAUN
          You sick fuck.

                              KURT
                         (beat)
          A nigger thought it up.

                              SHAUN
          What?

                              KURT
          A nigger thought up the black hole.

                              SHAUN
          I should shoot yo' ass now for lyin'.

                              KURT
          It's the truth. He helps us get
          other niggers out here.

                              SHAUN
          Who is it? What's his name?

                              KURT
          I don't know.

                              SHAUN
          I want his name.

                              KURT
          I said I don't know. Why would I
          protect a nigger?
                         (beat)
          Now what about my family?

          Shaun puts the gun to his chest and pulls the trigger.

                              SHAUN
          What about them?

     EXT. PAINTBALL FIELD/ THICK TWO - DAY

     Craig hears SHOTS and stumbles toward a tree, panting.

                              CRAIG
                         (whispering)
          Dear God.
                         (beat)
          Shaun.

     EXT. PAINTBALL FIELD/ THICK FOUR - DAY

     Steve and Doug are walking, looking for Black men.

                    STEVE
          I just came back from the house and
          Jerry said he wants us to get the
          nigger who brought them here too.

                    DOUG
          Who? Al? What for?

                    STEVE
          He didn't tell me. He only said for
          us to bring him back to the house
          when we catch him. He said he wanted
          him awake and not beat too bad.

                    DOUG
          You think Jerry's go'n kill him?

                    STEVE
          Prob'ly so.

                    DOUG
          What'd he do?

                    STEVE
          He's a nigger, Doug. What other
          reason do you need?

EXT. PAINTBALL FIELD/ THICK THREE - DAY

Shaun hears talking not far behind him. He climbs the tree
that he and Kurt fought under and adequately hides himself.
He perches himself in the tree, ready to strike. Steve and
Doug walk into his line of sight.

Shaun takes aim at Doug.

Steve and Doug step into blood covered leaves.

                    STEVE
               (looking down)
          What the fuck?

They follow the trail of blood on the leaves. The trail
leads them under the tree that Shaun is in. They SEE Kurt's
dead body.

                    DOUG
          Oh man. They got to Kurt!

                    STEVE
          Those fuckin' bastards!

Doug picks up the discarded wallet.

DOUG
They even robbed him.

STEVE
What'd you expect? They're niggers!
Fuckin' monkeys! It's in their
blood.

Doug searches around the body.

DOUG
Steve, I don't see Kurt's gun.

SHAUN
Here it is!

SERIES OF SHOTS

A) SHAUN SHOOTS DOUG IN THE STOMACH AND JUMPS ON STEVE. DOUG
DROPS HIS GUN.

B) STEVE SHOOTS SHAUN IN MID AIR. HE GOES DOWN HARD ON
STEVE.

C) STEVE PUSHES HIM OFF AND GETS UP. HE KICKS SHAUN'S GUN
AWAY. SHAUN LOOKS DEAD.

STEVE
Good move, monkey. Too bad it didn't
get you anywhere.

Shaun RAISES his head off the ground slowly.

SHAUN
(raspy voice)
Nowhere but on top of yo' ass.

STEVE
Not dead yet? Let's see if I can't
take care of that.

We SEE Steve get ready to pull the trigger. We HEAR a
gunshot and Steve falls dead to the ground. We SEE Craig
with the gun. Shaun drops his head on the ground and laughs
painfully.

SHAUN
I ain't never been so happy to see
anybody in my life!

CRAIG
I'm just glad I got here in time. I
thought you were dead. I heard
shots.

Craig helps Shaun sit up. Shaun is gasping for air and
moving slowly.

                         SHAUN
               Yeah, I took a couple of 'em out.
               There's somethin' crazy goin' on out
               here, man.

                         CRAIG
               You tellin' me?

                         SHAUN
               I mean, besides just killin' us.
               These fuckers are tryin' to kill
               Black folks in general.

                         CRAIG
               What are you talkin' about?

                         SHAUN
               Before I killed the first one, I made
               him tell me what the fuck was goin'
               on out here.

                         CRAIG
               How did you -

Shaun smiles.

                         CRAIG (cont'd)
                       (continuing)
               I don't even want to know.

                         SHAUN
               He told me that they call this place
               the black hole because they bring
               Black folks here and kill them.

                         CRAIG
               What?

                         SHAUN
               They were talkin' about round two or
               something like that. I heard another
               one talkin' about how this was his
               fifteenth game and thirty-second
               round, or something.

                         CRAIG
               That means we aren't the only game
               today.

                              SHAUN
                            (beat)
              Shit, man. You gotta get outta here.
              You gotta try and stop the others
              from coming out here and gettin'
              killed. They're tryin' to take us
              all out, C. You gotta stop those
              muthafuckas.

                              CRAIG
              You mean WE gotta get outta here and
              stop this madness.

                              SHAUN
                            (shaking his head)
              No, player. I mean you.

                              CRAIG
              Come on, man.

                              SHAUN
              Look, I'm busted up, man. All I'll
              do is slow you down.

                              CRAIG
              Yeah, but I'm not leavin' you here,
              man.

                              SHAUN
              You have to, if you want to get out.
              Go on.

                              CRAIG
              Shaun!

                              SHAUN
              Go on. I'll be okay. Don't worry
              'bout me. I'll find my way outta
              here if I have to kill every one of
              them before I do.

              Craig smiles.

                              SHAUN (cont'd)
                            (continuing)
              You just make sure you stop the other
              brothas from comin' out here.

              Shaun shakes Craig's hand. Craig is overwhelmed.

                              CRAIG
              Shaun, I -

                    SHAUN
         I know, man. Me too.

They embrace. Craig gives Shaun Doug's gun.

                    CRAIG
         If any of them come back here, shoot
         their asses.

                    SHAUN
         You ain't gotta tell me twice. Now
         go'n and get outta here, before I
         shoot your sorry ass, nigga.

                    CRAIG
         If I never hear that word again,
         it'll be too soon.

Craig stands up and looks at Shaun.

                    CRAIG (cont'd)
                  (continuing)
         Be safe, my brotha.

                    SHAUN
         You too.

Craig started to run off into the woods. Shaun calls out.

                    SHAUN (cont'd)
                  (continuing)
         Craig! I forgot! He said that one
         of us set this whole thing up.

                    CRAIG
         No.

                    SHAUN
         That's what he said. He could have
         been gassin' me. But watch your
         back.

                    CRAIG
         I'll keep the pizza warm for you,
         man.

                    SHAUN
         Keep the beer cold too, bra. Nobody
         likes warm beer. It tastes like
         piss.

Craig chuckles and runs into the woods.

EXT. DILAPIDATED HOUSE ON THE HILL - EVENING

The Old Man comes out of the house to find Wally, Chuck, and
Eddie sitting around talking.

                    THE OLD MAN
          What's goin' on? Where is that boy I
          told y'all to git?

                    EDDIE
          We ain't seen 'im yet. Steve's out
          lookin' for 'im right now.

                    THE OLD MAN
          I thought there was only two others
          left. What's all that shootin'?

Chuck laughs and looks at the guys.

                    CHUCK
          Sounds like our boys is out there
          havin' some fun.

The Old Man smacks Chuck in the back of the head.

                    THE OLD MAN
          You think somethin' is funny 'bout
          this, boy?

                    CHUCK
          What's the big deal? We'll get all
          of 'em and!

                    THE OLD MAN
          And then what? We'll go home and
          fuck our girls? We got another round
          to play here, boys!

Chuck looks away from The Old Man.

                    THE OLD MAN (cont'd)
                    (continuing)
          This shit's takin' too long. I want
          y'all to get up off your asses and
          git them three boys, you hear?

The Old Man hobbles back to the house. He looks up at the
darkening sky.

                    THE OLD MAN (cont'd)
          Hurry up. It's go'n rain soon.

EXT. PAINTBALL FIELD - NEUTRAL AREA ONE - EVENING

Craig runs to the edge of the woods. He SEES the cars. He
runs down to the Jetta, gun in hand, keeping his eyes open.
It starts to rain hard. He makes his way to the Cherokee
crouched and SEES Gary's corpse. Emotionally, he searches
Gary's pouch for the keys to the cars. He does not find
anything.

                    CRAIG
               Where are they?

In the b.g. the driver side door of the Jetta opens and Al
steps out. Al approaches behind Craig.

                    AL
               (jingling the keys)
          Are you looking for these?

Craig reaches for his gun but Al kicks it under the car.

                    AL (cont'd)
               (continuing)
          Turn around slowly.

Craig turns and faces him. He is visibly shocked.

                    AL (cont'd)
               (continuing)
          Good boy. Can you roll over and play
          dead too?

                    CRAIG
          You bastard! I can't believe it's
          you.

                    AL
          You look just like Martin did when he
          found out. I wonder if you'll look
          like he did just before he died.

                    CRAIG
          Why would you set us up? How could
          you be in this with them?

                    AL
          In this with them? You think I'm in
          cahoots with them? You don't know
          how wrong you are! I'm the one who
          started this whole thing! This is my
          brainchild, my baby.

We SEE Craig shaking his head.

AL (cont'd)
(continuing)
These backwater hicks couldn't come
up with an ingenious plan like this!

CRAIG
Why do you want to take out your own?

AL
I don't claim niggers as my own.

CRAIG
What?

AL
Niggers. You, Martin, the rest of
them. Y'all are niggers. We have
nothing in common. I work for a
living. You all take what I work for
and throw it away. So now it's time
for you to pay the price.

CRAIG
Do you hear yourself? You sound
crazy, man!

AL
Do I?

CRAIG
Yes! You're sick, man.

AL
You're right! I am sick. I'm sick
of working myself to death to be
recognized, only to be torn down at
the blink of an eye when one of you
comes around with your pants hanging
down below your underwear. I'm tired
of being called special because I
know how to annunciate my words.

We SEE Al's hand gripping the gun tightly.

AL (cont'd)
(continuing)
I'm tired of women clutching their
purses when I walk by because they
equate me with a punk like you
because my skin is black. I'm sick
of you car-jacking, crack-smoking,
nothing happening niggers ruining the
good life for me.

69.

                    CRAIG
          So you just gonna take us out so we
          don't get in your way anymore, is
          that the plan?

                    AL
          Right on. I'll take you out and
          these hicks'll take the blame for it.
          Just like they took the blame for
          Jerome and those thugs he was with in
          Chantilly. I am clean and free.

                    CRAIG
          What makes you think they'll let you
          get away with it?

                    AL
          Who? Those hicks?

                    CRAIG
          Yeah.

                    AL
          It's not a matter of me getting away
          with it. I've already gotten away
          with it.

                    CRAIG
          Is that why your boy got a gun on
          you?

Al's facial expression changes to concern. Eddie and Wally
are standing behind Al. Eddie has a rifle on Al.

                    AL
          What are you talking about?

                    EDDIE
          What a great speech. I'd clap if my
          hands wasn't full!
                    (smiling)
          - Throw down your gun.

Al drops his gun reluctantly. Wally goes over to Al and
picks up the gun. He walks behind Craig and puts his gun to
his back.

                    EDDIE (cont'd)
                    (continuing)
          Now, what was that shit you was
          talkin', boy?

                    AL
          Eddie, c'mon. I was settin' him up.
          I had to talk that way. It was the
          only way he would understand the
          intensity of this.

                    EDDIE
          Sounded like you was tryin' to pin
          the blame on us for all of this.

                    CRAIG
                    (mumbling)
          Sounded that way to me.

                    WALLY
          Shut the fuck up, boy!

     Al and Craig glare at each other.

                    AL
          No, that's not what was happening.

                    EDDIE
          I know what I heard. I don't take
          too kindly to people tryin' ta set me
          up. 'Specially no nigger.

                    AL
          Come on, Eddie. You know me better
          than that. This nigger's tryin' to
          make it seem like I was turning on
          you!

                    EDDIE
          That's not what was goin' on?

                    AL
          No! I want the same thing you want.
          That's why we did this whole thing.

                    EDDIE
          I don't much care what ya sayin',
          boy. I'd take your ass out right now
          if I hadn't promised you to Jerry.
          So if I was you, I'd save it for him.

                    AL
          Fine. Jerry and I will straighten
          this whole thing out.

                    CRAIG
          I bet you will.

                    EDDIE
          C'mon boys. Let's go.

Eddie puts the rifle in Al's back and pushed him along.
Wally does the same to Craig. They walk.

EXT. DILAPIDATED HOUSE ON THE HILL - RAINY EVENING

Eddie calls for Jerry when they get to the house. The rain
is really coming down now.

                    EDDIE
          Jerry!
                (beat)
          Jerry!
                (beat)
          I got a present for you!

Jerry comes out of the house with his gun. He looks at Al
and smiles.

                    JERRY
          Well, well, well. Look what the cat
          drug in.

Wally and Eddie start to laugh. Al is nervous.

                    AL
          Hey, man. I didn't know you were
          looking for me.

                    JERRY
          I know. That's part of the game. So
          what's this I hear about you blamin'
          us for your shit?

                    AL
          What are you talking about? I was
          only using that to get to Craig.

                    JERRY
          Oh, so you been mouthin' off again? I
          was talkin' about the shit you told
          Martin.

Al's eyes dart, trying to come up with a way out.

                    JERRY (cont'd)
                (continuing)
          Remember that? How we's nothin' but
          some dumb hicks and we's go'n take
          the fall for yo' backstabbin' plan.
          Ain't that what he said, Eddie?

Eddie is walking towards the house while he speaks. He
props his rifle on the house and sits down near the front
door.

                    EDDIE
          Yup. He was sayin' that same kinda
          shit to this nigger too.

                    AL
          You got it all wrong.

                    JERRY
          No, we got it just right. I ain't
          surprised. Once a lyin' back-
          stabber, always a lyin' back-stabber.

                    WALLY
          It's in their blood. Eddie told me
          he caught one of 'em gettin' in the
          car, leavin' his nigger friends.

                    EDDIE
          He didn't make it, though. He was
          beggin' and pleadin' for his life.
          Offered me money and everything. I
          bet he'd have sucked my dick if I'd a
          let him.

Eddie and Wally start to laugh. Wally is still standing
behind Craig with the gun in his back.

                    JERRY
          That's a nigger for you.

                    AL
          Come on, Jerry. What is this, huh? I
          thought we had a deal! Take this gun
          off me and shoot this nigger so we
          can get on with the game. We need to
          prepare for the second round.

                    JERRY
          You ain't got nothin' to prepare for
          'cept meetin' yo' maker.

                    AL
          Jerry, you can't mean that.

Jerry smiles at AL.

                    AL (cont'd)
                  (continuing)
          Come on Jerry, you need me.

JERRY
I need you? How's that?

AL
I can get you more of them. I can
lure them to the black hole. They'll
trust me. More niggers, Jerry. I
can get you big niggers, small
niggers, any kind of nigger you want.
I know you want to take them all out.
So do I.

JERRY
We been doin' this for years without
yo' help. What makes you think we
need you now?

AL
Look how smoothly this has been goin'
for us. No hassle, no fuss. I can
get them out here easily, without
them even questioning my motive.
Hell, these niggers don't even
realize I'm behind it until it's too
late.

JERRY
God, I hate niggers!

AL
So do I! I hate them as much as you
do. That's why this partnership will
work. I can get you all the niggers
you want, Jerry.

JERRY
What do you think you are to me?

Al's facial expression comes down from momentum to fear.

AL
(beat)
Don't do this, Jerry.

JERRY
Shut up, boy.

Jerry turns his back on Al.

AL
(shouting)
Jerry, don't do this!

Jerry turns around and points the gun at Al.

74.

                        JERRY
                Enjoy hell, nigger.

Jerry pulls the trigger. Al falls flat onto his back. His
head rolled to the side and faced Craig, eyes open. Al is
dead. Jerry turned and walked towards Craig.

                        JERRY (cont'd)
                    (continuing)
                How 'bout you? You ready to die,
                nigger?

Craig spits in Jerry's face.

                        CRAIG
                Fuck you.

Jerry turns his head with the hit. He wipes his face. He
punches Craig in the face and Craig goes down.

                        JERRY
                Wally, shoot this nigger.

                        WALLY
                With pleasure.

SERIES OF SHOTS

A) JERRY TURNS HIS BACK AND STARTS TO WALK AWAY AS WALLY
AIMS AT CRAIG.

B) A SHOT COMES FROM THE OPPOSITE HILL AND HITS WALLY IN THE
THROAT. HE GRABS HIS THROAT AND WE SEE BLOOD SPURT THROUGH
HIS FINGERS. HE IS DEAD.

C) CRAIG GETS WALLY'S GUN. HE LOOKS TO THE HILL AND SEES
SHAUN.

D) EDDIE GRABS HIS RIFLE AND AIMS. BEFORE HE CAN SHOOT AT
SHAUN, CRAIG SHOOTS HIM. HE IS DEAD.

E) JERRY SHOOTS SHAUN. SHAUN FALLS FORWARD AND OFF THE
HILL. HE IS DEAD.

F) CRAIG RUNS BEHIND THE HOUSE AND INTO THE WOODS.

G) JERRY SHOOTS AFTER HIM BUT MISSES.

                        JERRY
                Fuck!

Jerry runs into the house to get backup.

INT. DILAPIDATED HOUSE ON THE HILL - RAINY DAY

Jerry busts into the room. Brad is loading his rifle. Chuck
is looking out the window trying to find Craig. He has his
rifle raised on his shoulder. The Old Man is on the floor.

                    JERRY
          C'mon Brad. We might can catch him
          'fore he gets to the cars.

                    THE OLD MAN
          Don't matter anyway. We got their
          cars already.

                    BRAD
          That boy ain't goin' nowhere.

Jerry starts to smile.

                    JERRY
          Let's go get him, then.

EXT. PAINTBALL FIELD/ NEUTRAL AREA ONE - RAINY EVENING

Craig runs through the woods cautiously and quickly. He is
attacked by wayward bushes and he trips over downed tree
branches often. The rain is really coming down by this time
and his vision is impaired. He squints through the branches
at the spot where they had parked the cars.

The cars are gone. Only Gary's body remains. Craig runs
towards Gary's body bewildered. Craig SEES thick tire
marks. He squeezes his eyes shut, thinking. He SEES an
office with a light on. He SEES an old pick-up truck parked
on the side. Craig cocks his gun and approaches.

INT. ONE ROOM OFFICE - RAINY EVENING

Pete is closing up the paintball office. The office is moldy
and dank. It's more like a storage closet for the paintball
guns and ammo. He has a modest desk in there that is
splintering and a lock box where he keeps his money. He
counts the money and smiles. He puts the money back in the
lock box and packs that in his duffel bag.

                    PETE
          I always did like the smell of money.
          'Specially when it's mine!

Pete closes the bag with a chuckle and approaches the door.
He HEARS a noise on the right side of the office.

He stops and listens. When he hears nothing, he starts to
leave again. He HEARS the noise again.

                    PETE (cont'd)
                    (continuing)
             What the hell?

He puts his bag down and walks back to his desk to get a
rusted letter opener for protection. He creeps up on the
area with the letter opener gripped tightly in his right
hand. He leans forward, around the ammo boxes, cautiously.
The ammo boxes CAST a shadow on the wall that resembles that
of a tall human being. A cat jumps out, hissing as it runs
out of view.

                    PETE (cont'd)
                    (continuing;
                     relieved)
             Damn cat!

Pete drops his shoulders and lowers the letter opener. He
HEARS the rain and then turns slowly toward the open door.
The cat scampers out into the rain.

                    PETE (cont'd)
             I didn't open that door!

While Pete is facing the door in confusion Craig gets up
from behind the desk b.g. and approaches Pete silently.

He grabs him by the throat. He grabs Pete's right wrist and
turns the letter opener towards his eyes.

                    CRAIG
             No. I did.

Craig stabs Pete in the left eye with the rusty letter
opener. He grabs the keys to the pick-up truck off the
floor and puts them in his pocket. He exits.

EXT. ONE ROOM OFFICE - RAINY EVENING

Craig goes to the pick-up truck and is about to open the
driver's door when he HEARS rustling. He gets into the
flatbed and hides under the tarp. Brad and Jerry ar
slinking around the office. Jerry motions for Brad to go
around the pick-up truck.

INT. ONE ROOM OFFICE - RAINY EVENING

Jerry goes into the office. The lights are off and Jerry
can't see much in the semi-darkness.

                        JERRY
         Pete?
              (beat)
         Pete, you in here?

Pete's duffel bag is on the desk. Jerry goes to the desk. He
opens the duffel bag and removes the lock box. He shakes
his head in confusion as he fingers the lock box.

                        JERRY (cont'd)
                    (continuing)
         Pete, wouldn't leave his money out
         like this!
              (loud)
         - Pete? Where're you?

Jerry makes his way back to the light switch on the wall
cautiously. He turns on the light and he SEES splatters of
blood dripping down the dirty wall to the left of the desk.

                        JERRY (cont'd)
                    (continuing)
         Shit!

Jerry FOLLOWS the spray of the blood to the floor and SEES
Pete's mutilated body on the floor. The letter opener
protruding sickly from Pete's left eye socket.

There is blood and brain matter all over the floor and wall.
Jerry stumbles backwards.

                        JERRY (cont'd)
                    (continuing)
         I'll get you for this, nigger.

EXT. PICK-UP TRUCK - RAINY EVENING

Brad circles the front of the pick-up truck, crouching and
using the truck as a shield. He scours the woods looking
for a figure. He comes around the side of the pick-up
truck.

                        BRAD
         Come on out, nigger. It's over. You
         cain't get out. All yo' nigger
         friends is dead, boy. They went to
         hell, just like you will when I catch
         you.

INT. PICK-UP TRUCK/ FLATBED - RAINY EVENING

Craig lay silently under the tarp. He has the gun ready to
be fired. He can SEE Brad pacing in front of the flatbed
through a rip in the tarp. He waits.

EXT. PICK-UP TRUCK - RAINY EVENING

Brad walks a couple of steps away from the pick-up truck.
He crouches as he moves. Exasperated he stands tall facing
the woods.

                         BRAD
               Goddammit! Where are you, boy?

Craig gets up from the tarp fast.

                         CRAIG
               Right behind you.

Craig shoots Brad in the back of the head. Brad falls t the
ground, dead.

                         CRAIG (cont'd)
                         (continuing)
               If I was a snake, I'da bit yo' ass!

INT. DILAPIDATED HOUSE ON THE HILL - RAINY NIGHT

The Old Man and Chuck are in the house. They HEAR GUNSHOT.

                         CHUCK
               What the fuck is goin' on?

                         THE OLD MAN
               He's winning.

The Old Man hobbles over to the window.

                         THE OLD MAN (cont'd)
                         (continuing)
               This nigger just won't die.

                         CHUCK
               I'm goin' out there to end this shit
               right now.

                         THE OLD MAN
               Yes. You go do that. And bring me
               back a souvenir. He's the hardest
               buck we've had to break yet.

                        CHUCK
        But he will be broke. I'm go'n break
        him!
                (looking at his
                gun)
        - I'm go'n make him wish he wasn't
        born.

Chuck exits the room in a hurry. The Old Man is still
standing by the window looking out. He has a concerned look
on his face.

                        THE OLD MAN
        Do it.

EXT. PICK-UP TRUCK - RAINY NIGHT

Jerry exits the office as Brad hits the ground.

SERIES OF SHOTS

A) JERRY SHOOTS CRAIG IN THE ARM.

B) CRAIG ROLLS OFF THE FLATBED AND CROUCHES BEHIND THE
TRUCK.

C) CRAIG AIMS AND SHOOTS BUT THE GUN HAS RUN OUT OF BULLETS.
CRAIG LOOKS AT THE GUN IN DISBELIEF.

                        CRAIG
                (whispering)
        No. No fuckin' way.

Jerry starts laughing while he advances.

                        JERRY
        I heard that clicking, there, boy.
        Sounds like you shit outta bullets.
        That means you shit outta luck.

Craig drops the gun and sits still.

                        JERRY (cont'd)
                (continuing)
        You niggers sho' did give us a run
        today. But the run's over, boy.

Jerry walks slowly towards the end of the flatbed.

JERRY (cont'd)
(continuing)
You niggers are so stupid. You think
you know it all, you think you're
runnin' things, but you never are.
We're always on top. Like today. You
never had a chance.

Craig prepares himself to pounce.

JERRY (cont'd)
(continuing)
Even Al. He didn't have a chance in
hell. He thought he could trick us
into thinkin' we were in this
together. I ain't never wanted to be
in nothin' wit' no nigger in my life.
Y'all cain't do nothin' for me and my
kind. Y'all ain't even fit to shine
my shoes.

Jerry cocks his gun as he walks.

JERRY (cont'd)
(continuing)
So, I let him think what he wanted
to. As long as he was bringin' me
some bucks to kill, I had no problems
wit' 'im. But he wasn't never
gettin' out. He wasn't never go'n
come out on top. He got what was
comin' to 'im, what all y'all niggers
got comin' to ya.
(beat)
A long dance with the devil in hell.

Craig leaps from behind the pick-up truck.

CRAIG
You'll take my place, you bastard!

Craig pushes Jerry into the passenger side mirror, breaking
it off. Jerry drops the gun as he winces in pain. They
both stand and square off, each man is weaponless.

JERRY
You want to fight with me, boy?

CRAIG
A man's gotta do what a man's gotta
do.

                         JERRY
             Well, c'mon'n get some, then. I
             promise,
                  (beat)
             I'll make it quick.

SERIES OF SHOTS

A)   JERRY JABS AT CRAIG.

B)   CRAIG DUCKS IT AND KICKS JERRY IN THE STOMACH.

C)   JERRY DOUBLES OVER AND CRAIG HITS HIM ON THE BACK,

SENDING HIM TO THE GROUND.

                         CRAIG
             Get up!

Jerry rolls around holding his stomach and GROANING.

                         CRAIG (cont'd)
                  (continuing)
             Get up, man, you 'posed ta be so bad.
             Let's go!

Craig kicks Jerry in the ribs. Jerry is lifted off the
ground. He rolls when he lands.

                         CRAIG (cont'd)
                  (continuing;
                  leaning in to
                  Jerry)
             You ain't bad at all. Once you come
             out from behind that gun you ain't
             nothin'.

SERIES OF SHOTS

A)   JERRY FLINGS MUD INTO CRAIG'S EYES.

B)   CRAIG FLAILS BACKWARD, HIS HANDS GRABBING AT HIS EYES.

C)   JERRY RACES TOWARDS HIM AND TRIPS HIM.

D)   CRAIG FALLS TO THE GROUND HARD. JERRY PICKS UP A PIECE
OF BROKEN GLASS, GETS ON TOP OF CRAIG, AND STABS HIM IN THE
SHOULDER.

                         JERRY
             Niggers don't have no place in
             society and I'm go'n see to it that
             y'all is exterminated.

Jerry beats Craig while taunting him.

                    JERRY (cont'd)
                    (continuing)
          We don't need yo' kind messin' wit'
          our women and lurin' our children to
          drugs and disease.

We SEE Craig grab Jerry's fallen gun.

                    JERRY (cont'd)
                    (continuing)
          You niggers need to learn respect for
          the White Man.

Craig points the gun at Jerry.

                    CRAIG
          Respect this!

Craig shoots Jerry in the chest. He falls face first o
Craig. Craig shoves the body off him and gets up to run to
the pick-up truck. Jerry GRABS Craig's ankle, pulling Craig
to the ground. Craig LOOKS at Jerry in fear.

Jerry looks at Craig with dead eyes as his grip weakens and
his head PLOPS into the mud. He is dead. Craig kicks
Jerry's hand off him. He gets up and runs to the pick-up
truck.

INT. PICK-UP TRUCK - RAINY NIGHT

Craig gets in the front seat and pulls out the car keys. We
SEE several different keys on the loop.

                    CRAIG
          Oh, you've gotta be kidding me!

SERIES OF SHOTS

A) HURRIEDLY, CRAIG TRIES THE KEYS IN THE IGNITION.

B) CHUCK RUNS OUT OF THE BUSHES AND TAKES AIM AT

THE CRAIG'S HEAD. HE IS STANDING BEHIND THE PICK-UP

TRUCK.

C) WHILE CHUCK IS AIMING, CRAIG IS LOOKING FOR THE KEY.

HE TRIES A KEY IN THE IGNITION JUST AS CHUCK SHOOTS A

ROUND THAT BREAKS THE WINDSHIELD. CRAIG STAYS DOWN.

                    CRAIG (cont'd)
                  (whispering)
          Shit!

He starts looking for the right key frantically.

                    CHUCK
          Shit!

He cocks the gun and aims.

Craig finds the right key and turns the ignition. Without
looking up, Craig shifts the car into reverse and floors it.

Chuck is aiming at the driver's side of the truck. He SEES
the truck barreling toward him.

                    CHUCK (cont'd)
                  (continuing)
          Nooooooo!

The pick-up truck SLAMS into Chuck, flinging his body into
the air. It falls limply against a tree, dead.

Craig LOOKS at Chuck's broken body.

                    CRAIG
          Tough break.

EXT. ONE ROOM OFFICE/ ROAD- RAINY NIGHT

Craig leaves the office with his headlights off. He drives
past Gary's body and onto the approach road, cautiously.

                    CRAIG
          Please God. Let me get out of here.

Craig turns right onto the paved road.

                    CRAIG (cont'd)
                   (continuing)
               Yes!! Yes!!!

He LAUGHS gleefully in the car. He turns on the headlights
and speeds down the dark road.

INT. DILAPIDATED HOUSE ON THE HILL - RAINY NIGHT

The Old Man SEES the pick-up truck speed away from the
paintball field.

                    THE OLD MAN
          Damn.

The Old Man hobbles over to the phone. Dialing the rotary
dialer deliberately, the Old Man speaks roughly.

                    THE OLD MAN (cont'd)
                   (continuing)
               I need you ta git ready. One of 'em
               got out!
                   (listening)
               - I'll call it in. He just rode
               outta here in Pete's truck. I want
               that boy took down, you understand
               me?...
                   (turning,
                   looking out the
                   window)
               - And send in team two for the second
               round. Tell 'em to cut right to the
               chase this time.

The Old Man hangs up.

INT. PICK-UP TRUCK - NIGHT

Craig SEES the interstate signs up ahead. The rain has
stopped. He SMILES and speeds up. He SEES the sheriff's
department. Sloughing it off, he continues driving.

FLASHBACK:

EXT. PAINTBALL FIELD/ THICK THREE - DAY

                    SHAUN
               They were talkin' about round two or
               something like that.
                   (MORE)

                    SHAUN (cont'd)
          I heard another one talkin' about how
          this was his fifteenth game and
          thirty-second round, or something.

                    CRAIG
          That means we aren't the only game
          today.

                    SHAUN
                    (beat)
          Shit, man. You gotta get outta here.
          You gotta try and stop the others
          from coming out here and gettin'
          killed. They're tryin' to take us
          all out, C. You gotta stop those
          muthafuckas.

END FLASHBACK
                    CRAIG
          Shit.

Craig sighs and slams on the brakes, making a sharp U-turn.

INT. SHERIFF'S DEPARTMENT - NIGHT

Joe and BILL (43), the sheriff who is tall and lanky, sit in
the office. ANGIE (37), a prostitute, is in the holding
cell. She is wearing a hot pink cat suit with holes in the
rear and above the breasts. Joe is looking nervously at
Bill.

                    JOE
          Why don't you knock off for the
          night, Bill? I can lock up.

                    BILL
                    (not looking up)
          I still got a few thangs to take care
          of, 'fore I head home.

                    JOE
          You know Jill's waitin' on ya. She
          probably got a nice dinner cooked up
          for you and e'rythang.

Bill smiles, not looking up.

                    JOE (cont'd)
                    (continuing)
          I'll process this hooker for ya. Why
          don't you git on home to yo' pretty
          wife and show her a good time?

Bill looks up from his papers and over at the hooker in the
cell. He looks at Joe.

                    BILL
          Joe, if I didn't know better, I'd
          think you wanted me outta here so you
          could get a piece of ole Angie here.

                    ANGIE
          Ain't nothin' old 'bout Angie, baby.

                    JOE
          You talkin' crazy, Bill! I just
          want you to get some time wit' yo'
          wife, is all.

                    ANGIE
          Sure you do, baby. And my name is
          Alice. If you get him to leave,
          suga, I'll take you to wonderland for
          free.

Bill looks at his watch and sighs.

                    BILL
          I guess I should call it a night.
          Jill's been real sensitive lately.
          Been wantin' me home more.

                    JOE
          Maybe it's time you obliged.

Joe SMILES slyly. Bill gets up and takes his jacket off the
back of the chair.

                    BILL
          Maybe you're right, Joe.

The phone RINGS and Joe answers it. Bill collects his
things while Joe fields the phone call. Joe hangs up and
shakes his head.

                    BILL (cont'd)
                  (continuing)
          What was it?

                    JOE
          Ole Lady Parker's cat is stuck in a
          tree again.

                    BILL
          I swear, that cat must go up there
          three times a week! Damn, that's
          'cross town!
                  (MORE)

                    BILL (cont'd)
          There should be some other folks to
          call when shit like that happens.
          That ain't what the law is for.

                    JOE
          We lucky that's all they call us for.
          Beats havin' ta round up a bunch a
          dead bodies e'ry day and cain't find
          the killer or runnin' down drug
          dealers all night like they do in the
          city. Shoot, I'd rather take a cat
          out a tree any day than be dodgin'
          bullets.

                    BILL
          You got a point there.

Bill puts his jacket on and his sheriff's hat.

                    BILL (cont'd)
                    (continuing)
          I'm go'n go an get Ole Lady Parker's
          cat out the tree, and then I'ma go
          home and kiss my wife. Hell, I might
          do more than kissin'.

Joe laughs.

                    JOE
          You might indeed! See you, later,
          sheriff.

                    BILL
          You have a good night, Deputy. 'Night
          Angie. Git yo'self a good night's
          rest, 'fore the county come ta git
          cha in the mornin'.

Angie makes a face at Bill. Bill shuts the door laughing.

                    ANGIE
                    (looking at the door)
          I hope that cat scratches his eyes
          out!
                    (looking at Joe)
          - So what about you and me, suga? You
          want some of Angie's love potion? We
          could have a good time on this here
          cot, you know.

Joe goes into his desk drawer and takes out rubber gloves.
He puts them on and takes out a stolen gun and box of
ammunition. He loads the gun while Angie speaks.

                    ANGIE (cont'd)
                   (continuing)
        I could make it real sweet for you,
        baby. All you gotta do is let me go
        'fore the county come tomorrow. You
        ain't got to pay nothin' for this
        lovin', baby.

                    JOE
        Angie, you couldn't pay me to fuck
        you.

                    ANGIE
        You son of a bitch! When I get outta
        here, I'll report you to Bill for
        soliciting sex as a payoff.

                    JOE
        You would do 'ole Joe like that?

Joe points the gun at Angie.

                    ANGIE
        Okay Joe, take it easy. I was only
        kiddin' baby, you know that!

                    JOE
        I'm not.

She screams. He shoots her in the head. He turns the light
off in the cell.

INT. PICK-UP TRUCK - NIGHT

Craig pulls into the Sheriff department driveway and stops
the car. The sheriff's department is back from the road
with a wide dirt lot in front of it.

                    CRAIG
                   (getting out)
        I can't believe I'm doin' this.

INT. SHERIFF DEPARTMENT - NIGHT

Craig opens the door and SEES an amiable police officer
named Joe sitting behind his desk.

                    JOE
        Howdy son. How can I help you
        tonight?

                    CRAIG
          I want to report a murder. More than
          one. A lot, I guess.

Craig starts to shake as he thinks about his friends.

                    JOE
          A murder? Out here in Cheyenne
          County? You must got the wrong town,
          son. Don't nothin' like that happen
          out here. This town's quiet and God
          fearin'.

                    CRAIG
          I'm tellin' you. My friends were
          murdered at a paintball field up the
          road.

Craig is really trembling now. He begins to sweat.

                    JOE
          Take it easy, fella. Sit down. Relax
          a bit. Don't get yourself all worked
          up 'bout nothin'.

                    CRAIG
          Nothin'? I'm tellin' you that my
          friends were slaughtered in the woods
          and you're tellin' me that's nothin'?

He stands up and shoves the chair away from him with the
back of his legs.

                    CRAIG (cont'd)
                (continuing)
          I don't know why I even came here. I
          should just get the fuck outta this
          hick town.

Craig walks towards the door and opens it. Joe jumps to his
feet, still behind his desk. Joe is sweating.

                    JOE
          Hold on, now. I didn't say that
          you're friends being killed was
          nothin'. I was just saying that it's
          hard to believe something like that
          could happen here, is all. C'mon and
          sit back down. I wants to help ya
          sort this thang out.

                    CRAIG
          I know what happened and I know what
          I saw.

                    JOE
          And I believe that somethin' happened
          to you out here. Let's see if we
          can't figure it all out together.

Craig reluctantly shuts the door and walks back over to the
desk. He slouches down in the chair. He covers his face
with his hand and breathes deeply.

                    JOE (cont'd)
                 (continuing)
          Looks like you been through the
          ringer.

                    CRAIG
          You don't know the half.

                    JOE
          Tell me about it, son. I want to
          help.

                    CRAIG
          Okay, it's like this. These guys
          brought us out here on a dare to play
          paintball with them. We figured,
          what the hell? It was worth 100
          dollars so why not? When we get out
          here, though, they got real guns and
          we ain't got nothin' but paintballs
          to shoot.

Craig glances casually at the darkened cell.

                    CRAIG (cont'd)
                 (continuing)
          They took all my boys out, man. They
          killed them all. All but me.

                    JOE
          Good Lord! How'd you manage to
          escape?

                    CRAIG
          I almost didn't. They tried to take
          me out too, but I was able to -
                 (beat)
          ... I was lucky, man.

                    JOE
          I should say so! So what happened to
          them boys that brought y'all up here?

                    CRAIG
          They're dead. Some of 'em are,
          anyway.

                    JOE
          How many of 'em were there?

                    CRAIG
          Eight or ten.

                    JOE
          Did you get any of their names? Or
          did you notice any special marks on
          any of their bodies?

Craig SEES the rubber gloves and is suspicious.

                    CRAIG
          It's not like we were all one happy
          family out havin' a walk in the
          woods.

                    JOE
          I know, but I just wondered if you
          would be able to identify any of them
          if you had to. You know, the ones
          that are still alive.

                    CRAIG
          Maybe. But maybe not. Y'all good
          ole boys all look alike to me.

                    JOE
                 (beat)
          I'ma ignore that statement on account
          a what you been through.

Craig leans closer to Joe and puts his elbows on the desk.

                    CRAIG
          Look, I didn't mean that. It's
          just... Look, I came here to tell you
          that they're go'n do it again. And
          you gotta do somethin' to stop them.

                    JOE
          What?

                    CRAIG
          What don't you understand? They're
          going to do it again, man.

                    JOE
          Do what again?

CRAIG
They're plannin' on havin' another
round of this shit. They're go'n
have another game with some other
brothas. That's why I came here.
(beat)
I want to make sure that second game
never happens.

JOE
How do you know they plannin' another
game?

CRAIG
'Cause we heard some of them talkin'
'bout it. It's like they're tryin'
to exterminate us like rats or
somethin'. They're tryin' to take us
all out.

JOE
And when you say us, you mean who?

CRAIG
C'mon man! Black folks! They're
tryin' to wipe us out!

JOE
Okay, okay. So where is the other
team?

CRAIG
I don't know. I don't know who they
are. I just know that some more
brothas are comin' out here to play
this game. We can't let them go to
the paintball field.

Craig is getting upset again.

JOE
Okay, okay settle down.

Joe takes out a pen and paper and started to write.

JOE (cont'd)
(continuing)
What did you say your name was again?

CRAIG
Craig Johnson.

JOE
And where you from?

                    CRAIG
Washington, DC. What does this have
to do with anything?

                    JOE
Just a formality.

                    CRAIG
We don't have time for the
formalities. We gotta get out there
and put up a barricade or something.
We can't let those guys go in there
to get killed.

                    JOE
Now, suppose what you're sayin' is
true!

                    CRAIG
Suppose? It is true! You think I
could make up some wicked shit like
this?

                    JOE
I didn't say I didn't believe ya, but
what I'm tryin' to get my mind around
is, if what you're sayin' is true,
then what you think I'm go'n do 'bout
it?

                    CRAIG
What?

                    JOE
There ain't no law 'gainst huntin'
out here in Cheyenne County, boy!

                    CRAIG
You're one of them!

                    JOE
'Specially when you got dirty animals
trespassin' on yo' property. Hell,
way I see it, they's just exercisin'
they're God given right to protect
they land. You want me to prosecute
a man for protectin' his land, boy?

Craig jumps up to leave but Joe points his gun at him.

                    JOE (cont'd)
                 (continuing)
What's your hurry, boy? We was just
startin' ta understand each other.

Craig glares at him.

                    JOE (cont'd)
                 (continuing)
          Sit down a spell. We ain't finished
          yet.

Craig remains standing.

                    JOE (cont'd)
                 (continuing)
          I said sit down, nigger. Don't make
          me have to tell you again.

Craig sits slowly, not taking his eyes off Joe or the gun.

                    JOE (cont'd)
                 (continuing)
          Good boy. Now, let's talk some more
          about what you say you saw.

                    CRAIG
          Why? Ain't like anybody else's go'n
          hear about it but you.

                    JOE
                 (smiling)
          You got a point there. But I'd like
          to hear about how they killed yo'
          friends. How they shot them down
          like dogs, every one of 'em. I wanna
          know if they hollered and how loud,
          if they did. I wanna know if they
          begged for their lives.

                    CRAIG
          I wouldn't give you the satisfaction
          of knowing.

Joe reclines in his chair. He points the gun at Craig
loosely.

                    JOE
          You got a smart mouth, you know that,
          boy? I oughta kick yo' ass right now
          for mouthin' off to me.

                    CRAIG
          You and what army?

                    JOE
                 (laughing)
          Don't you know you go'n die tonight,
          boy? Ain't nobody go'n save you.
                 (MORE)

                    JOE (cont'd)
      All yo' nigger friends is dead and
      you out here all by yo'self.

Joe gets up and puts the gun in Craig's face.

                    JOE (cont'd)
                   (continuing)
      I already got my story together on
      how I came to have two dead bodies in
      my station on a Saturday night.

Craig looked at Joe, confused.

                    JOE (cont'd)
                   (continuing)
      You wonderin' how I came to two? Let
      me introduce you to Angie, the town
      slut.

Joe walks over to the light switch and turns on the light in
the cell. We SEE Angie laying in a puddle of blood.

                    JOE (cont'd)
                   (continuing)
      She was goin' to county tomorrow, but
      I guess she won't be makin' that
      trip.

He walks back to Craig.

                    JOE (cont'd)
                   (continuing)
      See, the way I'll tell it, you came
      in here totin' this here gun.

He SHOWS Craig the gun.

                    JOE (cont'd)
                   (continuing)
      You made me open Angie's cell and
      then you tied me up. But seein' as
      yous a nigger, you cain't tie a
      decent knot to save your life. You
      went in the cell wit' Angie and tried
      to rape her, but she resisted you.
      So you shot her in the head. By that
      time I had got out my ropes and I
      warned you to put yo' gun down. You
      wouldn't do it, though!
                   (pacing)
      - No, you wouldn't comply. Then you
      turned yo' gun on me. So I was
      forced to do the only thing I could
      do. I shot you...
                   (MORE)

                         JOE (cont'd)
                      (putting the gun
                      (to Craig's head)
            - Bang!

Craig jumps.

                         JOE (cont'd)
                      (continuing)
            What's a matter boy? You right jumpy
            tonight!

                         CRAIG
            Fuck you.

Joe chuckles.

                         JOE
            That's the story as I see it. That's
            what I'm puttin' in my report about
            Craig Johnson.

Joe holds up the scrap paper that he took notes on and
shakes it in the air.

                         JOE (cont'd)
                      (continuing)
            That's what they go'n believe.

Joe pats Craig on the shoulder as he walks behind his chair.
Craig shrugs his hand off.

                         JOE (cont'd)
                      (continuing)
            Get on up boy. We got to do this
            right.

Joe pushes Craig's shoulder with the gun. Craig walks to
the cell door on Joe's lead. Craig looks at Angie and
cringes.

                         JOE (cont'd)
                      (continuing)
            Don't worry 'bout that, boy. You
            won't see nothin' in a few minutes.

Joe stands away from Craig.

                         JOE (cont'd)
                      (continuing)
            Move a little to your left.

Craig stands still.

                    CRAIG
          I'm not go'n help you set up my
          murder.

                    JOE
          It don't really matter. I'm the only
          witness to it. Who else they go'n
          believe?

Craig licks his lips, trying to think of a way to get out of
this situation.

                    JOE (cont'd)
                 (continuing)
          Say goodbye, nigger.

Joe points the gun at Craig and starts to pull the trigger.
Bill opens the office door.

                    BILL
                 (looking down)
          Joe, I got out there and that cat
          wasn't in the tree at all. As a
          matter of fact, wasn't a soul...

Bill pauses as he finally looks up and sees what is going
on.

                    BILL (cont'd)
                 (continuing)
          ... In the place.

He quickly draws his gun and points it at Craig.

                    BILL (cont'd)
                 (continuing)
          Joe, what in the hell is goin' on
          here?

                    JOE
          This nigger busted in here and shot
          ole Angie. He was tryin' to rape her
          when I got my gun on 'im.

                    CRAIG
                 (to Bill)
          I'm unarmed, man.

                    BILL
          I'm the Sheriff of this damn town,
          you betta damn well respect that,
          boy!

                    CRAIG
        I'm unarmed, Sheriff. I came in here
        to report a murder, not commit one.

                    BILL
        A murder? What you talkin' about,
        boy?

                    CRAIG
        My friends were murdered at the
        paintball field...

                    BILL
        Pete's place?

                    JOE
        Don't listen to this nigger, Bill.
        I'm tellin' you he shot Angie and he
        attacked me.

                    BILL
        What do you mean, he attacked you?

                    JOE
        He tied me up after he made me open
        the cell door. He wanted to rape
        Angie. When she wouldn't let him
        touch her, he hauled off and shot her
        in the head. I had just 'bout got my
        ropes untied when he, when this
        bastard nigger killed her. I had just
        wrassled the gun away from 'im when
        you came in.

Bill grabs Craig by the shirt and threw him into the chair
by Joe's desk.

                    BILL
        Sit down, you punk. This'll be the
        last stunt you ever pull. I'm gonna
        make sure you go up shit's creek for
        this.

Bill pistol whips Craig as he sits in the chair. Craig is
knocked semi-unconscious. Joe sits down behind his desk and
smirks at Craig. He searches for the cell key.

Bill walks over to his desk and GLANCES at the floor near
Joe's desk. There is no rope. Concerned, Bill walks around
the back end of his desk and LOOKS behind Joe's desk.

No rope.

He looks at Joe. Joe is sweating profusely and he has a sly
look on his face.

Bill looks at Craig and believes him.

Quietly, Bill COCKS his gun.

                        BILL (cont'd)
                      (continuing)
            Joe, why don't you lock that boy up
            in the cell with Angie. When he
            wakes up he'll be sitting in her
            blood. Make 'im think about what he
            done.

                        JOE
            I will. I'm just...

                        BILL
            Lookin' for the cell key?
            Joe is silent. He keeps looking.
                      (continuing)
            I thought you said that boy made you
            open the cell door so he could get at
            Angie.

Joe keeps his head down. Craig is starting to come to.

                        BILL (cont'd)
                      (continuing)
            Just before he tied you up.

Joe stops looking for the key. He stares at Craig who is in
and out of consciousness. Joe takes a deep breath.

                        JOE
            It didn't have to be this way, Bill.
                      (beat)
            It didn't have to be this way.

SERIES OF SHOTS

A) JOE TURNS QUICKLY AND SHOOTS BILL IN THE STOMACH.

B) AT THE SAME TIME, BILL SHOOTS JOE IN THE CHEST.

C) AS THEY BOTH FALL CRAIG JUMPS OUT OF THE CHAIR AND STAGGERS OUT TOWARD THE PICK-UP TRUCK.

EXT. RURAL MARYLAND ROAD - NIGHT

A sports utility truck and a sedan are traveling the road to the paintball field. The occupants are all Black men.

INT. SPORTS UTILITY TRUCK - NIGHT

Four men are in the sports utility truck. AD LIB music from a tape. The passenger (DEREK) turns the reading light on and reads the directions in mumbles. One of the guys in the back is sleeping and the other guy in the back is looking out of the window. Their names are DEREK, NATHAN, CHRIS, and TIM. All are dressed in sweats. Following behind them in the sedan are ANTOINE, Black Man #1 and Black Man #2.

                    DEREK
          Okay, okay. According to the
          directions, we're on the right road.

Nathan is shaking his head and patting the steering wheel to the beat of the music.

                    NATHAN
          Good. This is no time to be gettin'
          lost. It's dark as hell out this
          muthafucka.

                    CHRIS
          Whose bright idea was it to play
          paintball at night?

                    DEREK
          What the fuck is paintball anyway?

                    NATHAN
          Ask the nigga snorin'. This is his
          shit, rememba?

                    CHRIS
          Tim's crazy ass. I wouldn't be
          surprised if he didn't find this
          thing on the Internet.
                              (MORE)

                    CHRIS (cont'd)
          You know he's becoming a bigger geek
          as the years go by.

                    DEREK
          I thought he said he heard about it
          from some college buddy. Some guy
          named Al.
          Chris shrugs his shoulders.

     EXT. SHERIFF'S DEPARTMENT - NIGHT

     Craig runs out of the sheriff's department and SEES the
     headlights coming up the street. He starts to wave his
     hands while he approaches the edge of the road.

     SERIES OF SHOTS

     A) JOE STUMBLES OUT OF THE OFFICE AND AIMS HIS GUN,

     SHOOTING CRAIG WHILE GASPING FOR AIR.

     B) CRAIG GETS SHOT IN THE SHOULDER JUST AS THE TRUCK

     AND SEDAN CRUISE BY THE OFFICE. CRAIG FALLS TO THE

     GROUND, UNCONSCIOUS.

     C) JOE FALLS TO THE GROUND AND DIES.

     INT. SPORTS UTILITY TRUCK - NIGHT

     The music is loud in the sports utility truck. They hear a
     BOOM outside.

                    NATHAN
               (turning the
               radio down)
          Did y'all hear somethin'?

                    CHRIS
          Sounded like a tire blowing out.

                    TIM
          Or Antoine and them niggas fartin'.

     They laugh. Tim yawned loudly and stretched.

                    DEREK
          Welcome back to the land of the
          livin', partner.

                         CHRIS
                      (effeminately)
                 Are you ready for your paintball
                 excursion?

                          TIM
                 Y'all need to loosen up. Get into
                 it. It sounded like fun, the way Al
                 pumped it up. Goggles, helmets with
                 lights on the brim, toy guns. It's
                 like the war games we used to play
                 when we were kids.

                         NATHAN
                 You mean what you used to play. Where
                 I come from you don't tote no gun,
                 unless you plan on usin' it.

                          TIM
                 You'll see. Plus, there's 100
                 dollars in it if we win. It's easy
                 money.

                         CHRIS
                 Yeah, I'm getting my money either
                 way. Win, lose, or draw.

                         DEREK
                 How's that?

                         CHRIS
                 If we do anything other than win, I'm
                 taking my share out Tim's ass!

     They laugh.

     INT. CONTEMPORARY PICK-UP TRUCK - NIGHT

     JAKE and WAYNE are riding in the two door truck. RICH is
     riding on the flatbed and listening through the back window.
     They are coming up the same dark road that the Black guys
     are, but from the other direction.

                         JAKE
                 Damn, man. You know The Old Man's
                 go'n kick our asses fo' bein' late.

                         WAYNE
                 It ain't our fault they called so
                 late. I wasn't even fixin' ta play
                 tonight.

                          JAKE
         I guess that first batch was more
         than Jerry and his boys could handle.
         They laugh.

                          WAYNE
         I'll bet them bucks tore them boys a
         new asshole.

                          RICH
         Yeah, Jerry's boys was always weak.

                          RICH
         I tol' The Old Man they couldn't
         handle this kind of work. They never
         had the backbone for it.

                          JAKE
         The problem is they was busy tryin'
         to be fancy wit' this. Bringin' 'em
         out here to play paintball instead of
         just takin' them out.

                          WAYNE
         Yeah, like we go'n do.

                          JAKE
         We'll show him what we can do. These
         boys ain't go'n be nothin' fo' us.
         An' then maybe The Old Man'll let us
         run the rest of the rounds.

                          WAYNE
         Speak 'a the devil.
         Wayne points at the two cars
         approaching them. Jake
         puts on his bright lights.

    INT. SPORTS UTILITY TRUCK - NIGHT

                          NATHAN
         Damn! Why do people have to be so
         annoying. He's got his brights on
         like he can't see me coming.

                          CHRIS
         Nate, we're a bunch of Black men in a
         black truck in the black of night
         wit' yo' midnight blue black ass
         behind the wheel. Maybe he can't see
         us.

    They laugh.

                    DEREK
        Nate, man. I think this is it. I
        see a sign on the ground!
                (squinting, reading
                aloud slowly)
        - Pete's Paintball. I think that's
        it.

                    CHRIS
        A mind is a terrible thing to waste,
        my brotha. I think you might want to
        go back and brush up on your phonics.

                    DEREK
        I think you might want to kiss my
        ass.

                    CHRIS
        Kick? Maybe. Kiss? Never.

They laugh as Nathan makes a left onto the muddy road that
leads to Pete's Paintball.

INT. CONTEMPORARY PICK-UP TRUCK - NIGHT

Jake, Wayne, and Rich watch the Black men turn into Pete's
Paintball field. Jake turns off his high beams.

                    JAKE
        There they go.

                    RICH
        In their souped up cars.

                    WAYNE
        Easy prey.

                    RICH
        Where's Will and them boys from town?
        There's more of 'em than us.

                    WAYNE
        They'll be comin' along soon. I tole
        'em to meet us here. Don't worry,
        they won't miss it. They want a
        piece of these niggers as much as we
        do.

                    JAKE
        C'mon y'all. Let's catch us some
        niggers.

They get excited about the conquest as Jake turns into
Pete's Paintball field.

INT. DILAPIDATED HOUSE ON HILL - NIGHT

The Old Man looks at his watch and then back out of the
binoculars he is holding.

EXT. PAINTBALL FIELD/ NEUTRAL AREA ONE - NIGHT

The Black guys get out of their cars and look around. It is
pitch black out, not a light in sight, except for the dim
glint up on a hill coming from the dilapidated house.

                    ANTOINE
          Where the fuck is the light switch?

                    NATHAN
          Yeah, I wonder where the other team
          is.

                    CHRIS
          Maybe we should drive up the hill
          some more. There's a light on up
          there. Maybe we stopped too soon.

                    NATHAN
          Do you see the mud out here? We'd
          sink if we kept going.

                    DEREK
          Tim, this is your gig. Where's your
          boy Al?

                    TIM
          I don't know. He told me he'd meet
          us at the first neutral area, which
          I'm assuming is this.

Tim LOOKS down at the tracks in the mud.

                    TIM (cont'd)
                  (continuing)
          Somebody's been here, though.at the
          tracks. It looks like Looks like
          somebody tore outta here on a
          mission.

Tim starts to walk towards the tracks near the office. We
SEE Chuck's body slumped at the base of a tree ahead, just
out of Tim's view.

106.

INT. DILAPIDATED HOUSE ON THE HILL - NIGHT

The Old Man is looking through the binoculars at Tim
approaching the office.

                    THE OLD MAN
          Slow down, nigger. You go'n start
          the game off on the wrong foot.

EXT. PAINTBALL FIELD/ NEUTRAL AREA ONE - NIGHT

The contemporary pick-up truck pulls up the drive with its
lights off. When it reaches the Black men, the bright
lights turn on.

INT. DILAPIDATED HOUSE ON THE HILL - NIGHT

The Old Man sees the White men pull up in their truck.

He begins to laugh in a raspy voice.

                    THE OLD MAN
          Curiosity killed the cat.
               (beat)
          And a few niggers too.

EXT. PAINTBALL FIELD/ NEUTRAL AREA ONE - NIGHT

Tim stops walking toward the office and turns to the pick-up
truck. They all shield their eyes from the bright light.

                    DEREK
               (low)
          What the fuck is this?

Jake, Wayne, and Rich get out of the truck. They stroll
slowly towards the Black men. They have cocky smiles on
their faces. Rich is carrying a rifle. The Black men are
looking at the White men in confusion. They have their eyes
shielded from the light and are trying to make out who is
approaching them.

                    JAKE
          Did you boys come out here to play
          paintball?

EXT. PAINTBALL FIELD/ NEUTRAL AREA ONE AERIAL - NIGHT

Jake, Wayne and Tim stand off in front of the Black men. A
second contemporary truck pulls up and blocks the exit area.

Four White men jump out. O.S. of the rifles cocking. The
Black men split up and start to run.

INT. DILAPIDATED HOUSE ON THE HILL - NIGHT

The Old Man is standing in the window looking at the scene
through his binoculars. He is smiling as he watches the cat
and mouse game being set up on the paintball field. We HEAR
a SHOT and the scene goes BLACK.

Voice Over of The Old Man laughing in a raspy voice.

                    THE OLD MAN (V.O.)
               Let the games begin.

EXT. SHERIFF'S DEPARTMENT/WOODS - MORNING

Derek is dirty. He is running through the woods looking
over his shoulder in fear. He has blood on his shirt and he
is limping. He stops at the edge of the woods and peers
out. He SEES the sheriff's station. Scouring the area, he
runs towards it, crouched.

EXT. SHERIFF'S DEPARTMENT - MORNING

Craig rolls over onto his back slowly. He cringes in pain.
He squeezes his eyes shut as he touches the dried blood on
his shoulder. Derek approaches the body on the ground
slowly.

                    DEREK
                    (whispering)
               Hey, man.

Craig doesn't answer. Derek gets on one knee and leans down
to his face.

                    DEREK (cont'd)
                    (continuing)
               Hey, man.

Craig opens his eyes quickly and backs away in fear.

                    DEREK (cont'd)
                    (continuing)
               It's okay, it's okay. I won't hurt
               you.

Craig sighs with relief.

                        CRAIG
            Are you one of the brothas from the
            truck last night?
                        DEREK
        Yeah.

                        CRAIG
            Where's the rest of your crew?

    Derek looks down as he speaks.

                        DEREK
        They!
                (beat)
            - I'm the only one who made it out,
            man. They're tryin' to kill us!

                        CRAIG
            I know, man. They got us too.

    They look towards the woods.

                        CRAIG
                (continuing)
            How'd you get out, man?

    Derek is still looking towards the woods while he answers
    Craig.

                        DEREK
            No offense, man, but I'd rather hold
            off on the small talk until we're
            hell and gone from here.

                        CRAIG
            I hear you.

    Craig struggles to get up. Derek helps him to his feet.

                        DEREK
            Are you all right, man? Can you run?

                        CRAIG
            I'll make it. My ride is right
            there.

    Craig points at Pete's PICK-UP TRUCK. Derek LOOKS at the
    beat up truck and chuckles. LONG SHOT on their backs as
    they jog towards the pick-up truck through a tracking lens.

                        DEREK (V.O.)
            Tell me you stole that from one of
            them.

                          CRAIG (V.O.)
                  What if I didn't?

Derek laughs.

                          DEREK (V.O.)
                  Don't tell me that, man.

We SEE a White male aiming a shotgun at Craig and Derek from
a hiding spot in the bushes. He is watching them jog toward
the pick-up truck through the viewfinder mounted on the
firearm. We HEAR him chuckle and he starts to pull the
trigger.

BLACKOUT as the trigger is pulled and we HEAR a SHOT.

FADE OUT.

ABOUT L. MARIE WOOD

L. Marie Wood is an award-winning psychological horror author and screenwriter. She won the Golden Stake Award for her novel The Promise Keeper. Her screenplays have won Best Horror, Best Afrofuturism/Horror/Sci-Fi, and Best Short Screenplay awards at several film festivals. Wood's short fiction has been published widely, most recently in *Slay: Stories of the*

Vampire Noire and Bram Stoker Award Finalist anthology, *Sycorax's Daughters*.

Learn more about her at www.lmariewood.com.

Made in the USA
Middletown, DE
16 March 2022

62783308R00099